ROAR
OF THE
DARK

Aastha Rathod Naad is an emerging creator who started her journey in 2017 with the television show *Aisi Deewangi Dekhi Nahi Kahin*, which she produced for Zee TV as well as the Hindi feature film, *MA Pass*. She then went on to produce many web-series like *Poison*, *Bhoot Purva* and *Bhram* for Zee5 and the Hindi feature film, *1920: Horrors of the Hearts*.

Trained in classical vocal music from Prayag Sangeet Samiti, Prayagraj, she aspires to tell stories that are layered and intentionally located on the fringes of society—stories that jolt both our perception and conscience. This book is just the beginning in unravelling forbidden realities; many more are still waiting to be uncovered.

ROAR
OF THE
DARK

AASTHA RATHOD NAAD

RUPA

Published by
Rupa Publications India Pvt. Ltd 2024
7/16, Ansari Road, Daryaganj
New Delhi 110002

Sales centres:
Bengaluru Chennai
Hyderabad Jaipur Kathmandu
Kolkata Mumbai Prayagraj

Copyright © Aastha Rathod Naad 2024

The views and opinions expressed in this book are the
author's own and the facts are as reported by her which
have been verified to the extent possible, and the publishers
are not in any way liable for the same.

All rights reserved.
No part of this publication may be reproduced, transmitted,
or stored in a retrieval system, in any form or by any means,
electronic, mechanical, photocopying, recording or otherwise,
without the prior permission of the publisher.

P-ISBN: 978-93-5702-987-2
E-ISBN: 978-93-5702-909-4

First impression 2024

10 9 8 7 6 5 4 3 2 1

The moral right of the author has been asserted.

Printed in India

This book is sold subject to the condition that it shall not,
by way of trade or otherwise, be lent, resold, hired out, or otherwise
circulated, without the publisher's prior consent, in any form of
binding or cover other than that in which it is published.

*I dedicate this book to my lifelines—my isht,
Mahadev; my mother, Santosh Rathore; father,
Raghuvendra Singh Rathore; brother, Ajay Singh Rathore
and my beloved companion, Jatin Sethi!*

My dreams are able to fly because they fuel my wings!

Contents

1. Judgement Day — 1
2. Meera Arrives in Mumbai — 6
3. Meera Meets Joe and Kalika — 16
4. The Morning after the Party — 34
5. Kalika Explores the Forbidden World — 36
6. Beyond Her Wildest Dreams — 62
7. Meera Meets Maheen — 66
8. Veer Tries to Woo Meera — 84
9. Roar of the Dark — 91
10. Kalika Begins a New Chapter — 107
11. Joe Burns for Redemption — 114
12. Maheen Is Engulfed by the Dark — 125
13. A New Reality for Meera — 139
14. Meera Dares the Unthinkable — 176
15. Time to Face the Music — 178
16. My Last Scream — 184
17. Meera Meets Mahadev — 191

Acknowledgements — *195*

Judgement Day

5 March 2012

The scene outside is horrifying. Fires are ablaze and thick black smoke slowly envelops me in a dense darkness. The strong pungent odour in the air repulses me as I struggle to breathe. Is this how it smells when corpses are burnt? I can hear the mob screaming; their cries sound desperate, disgruntled, deafening.

It is dark where I am sitting. The marble floor of my living room feels colder than ever as I try to drown out the commotion. It is a wasted effort, as the cries filter in through the closed windows and doors, breaking me into a thousand pieces. Is this the hell they described in Hindu mythological scriptures? Perhaps today is the last day of my life, and these breaths are my last. The screams will eventually invade my home, stab my chest and render me lifeless.

On the glass table facing the sofa is a marble statue that Veer, my fiancé, had got for me—a naked woman sitting on the back of an eagle as the mighty bird takes to the skies. I remember the day he had brought it home. Almost strategically, he had placed it next to a photograph from the day we had first met.

'It is art, you know, precious art,' Veer had remarked. 'I paid five thousand rupees for it. There's something unique about it.'

I had smiled sarcastically. 'If she had been clothed, you might have got it for five hundred rupees. But then, it wouldn't have been precious art, no?'

'Can't you rise above the nudity?' Veer had rolled his eyes, obviously annoyed.

The two of us had stared at each other for a while, listening to unspoken words. I wonder what he would have thought if he had been able to read my mind that day.

※

I live in a rented two-bedroom flat on the twentieth floor of Bhoomi Cooperative Society, one of the many residential buildings in Bandra, Mumbai. Veer had picked the apartment for me. We were only going to use it as a temporary accommodation until we got married. My parents were dead set against the idea of us living together before tying the knot.

After I moved in, I laboured to spruce up the apartment. I hung thin grey curtains in the living room to mute the saffron sunlight of the morning. I stitched them with love, along with seat covers and cushions for the black sofa. Veer, who had always been drawn to black, resisted my efforts to bring some colour to the place. An obnoxious work of 'modern art' hung on the wall, made with some of the darkest colours in the palette. I was surprised at how we both loved the shades of grey and black. I wondered if Veer had had a premonition of the things to come. Was this why he had decorated our home with shades that were the colour of night?

The mob outside my building is getting wilder. Do they want to hear my shrieks? Perhaps they are agitated because I am still hopeful, despite burning for so long in shame and guilt. What the mob doesn't know is that I have failed, but I have not been defeated.

The ringing phone brings me back from my reverie. I have no idea how long it has been ringing.

'Hello, Ma,' I say, my voice trembling but cautious. It would never do for Ma to sense that I had been crying. 'Why do you sound so tense? I am twenty-four! I can look after myself.'

Ma is frazzled. She goes on breathlessly about the reports on all major news channels. 'Turn off the television, Ma,' I try to calm her. 'That can't be my flat you see on the screen. There's no mob here. The news channels must be talking about another Meera. Your daughter isn't the only Meera around, you know!'

It isn't easy to distract Ma when she gets anxious about me. She asks about my unsteady voice. When was I coming home? 'Tomorrow,' I reply. 'I will be home tomorrow, Ma. Everything is fine. I just have a slight cold.'

Ma relents for the time being. I assure her that I will keep my door closed. Lying to Ma makes me feel distinctly unsettled; I have never done it before. Did my undoing begin when I first left Rishikesh, my hometown, and arrived in Mumbai six months ago? The last six months have completely changed my life. They have taken away everything I valued—my dreams, peace, desires and the belief system which had kept me breathing since I was born.

There was a time when I, Meera Thakur, met the day with the sun in my eyes and welcomed every morning with hope. I was attuned to my inner voice and followed my heart; nothing unnerved me. But in only six months, I have become a mere shadow of my former self. The Meera of today is distrusting and suspicious; clouds of disbelief shroud even the steeliest truths of my life. Night-time petrifies me the most. I shake in fear when darkness envelops the world each day. What a long way I have come from being in love with the dark, from worshipping Mahadev—the dark lord!

Today is a special day. The year is 2012, and it is 5 March.

Today is the day when Veer and I were supposed to get married. The wedding cards had been printed. Tents would have been erected for the ceremony. But all of that was before. Before my life changed forever...

In these six months, I became friends with Maheen, Joe and Kalika. I shall forever cherish the memories we made together. As I lie quietly on the cold floor of my living room, I wonder what they are doing. Has Maheen drawn back the curtains? She must be frightened of the mob raging outside our building. Will Joe ever forgive me? Can I ever make it up to Veer for causing misery to Joe, his best friend? Will Kalika also become a victim of this manic mob? Will we ever forget that cursed night that altered our lives forever? That night, while the world celebrated the start of a new year, the four of us prepared for the death of our old selves.

I had come to Mumbai with a superiority complex. I believed that I had the key to every lock and enough magic to bring light to any dark corner. For six months I knocked persistently on many doors, but they remained shut invariably. I persevered tirelessly because my pride would not let me give up. Drenched in a feeling of supremacy, I wanted to see a world which *I* approved of. I wanted to rewrite destinies. I realized the futility of my endeavour much too late. Only the one who had locked the door could unlock it. The rise of the dark was inevitable. It's roar was deafening. I decided to leave all fear behind. I would take my truth and forge on in the world.

'*Satyamev Jayate*'—isn't that what they say? Truth alone conquers. Why don't they say '*Satyamev Jiyate*'? That truth alone lives? I think it is because the truth is all-conquering, but not immortal. Will I live to see the rising sun of tomorrow? Will I live to make a new beginning?

Meera Arrives in Mumbai

1 October 2011

People moved about busily at the main entrance of Sharmila Publications. The imposing high-rise glass building almost resembled a palace. Surely, the owner must feel no less than a queen. One of the most prominent publishing houses in Mumbai, Sharmila Publications was helmed by Sharmila Tejwal, who, as reported by a local daily, was 'a boon to budding writers'.

As I stared at the towering forty-storeyed building, I felt a growing inferiority complex. I glanced down at myself; everything about me screamed 'small town'. I was wearing a yellow cotton skirt and a red *kurti*, loose at the waist but tight around my wrists. I had accessorized my outfit with red bangles, red shoes, a glasswork bag and a thin golden nose ring. The shoes I was wearing were the costliest pair in the main market in Rishikesh—nearly five hundred rupees.

'Do I look fit for an interview?' I asked my small pocket-mirror. My complexion was fair; my brown eyes were lined in black. I had a round face, thin lips, an ordinary nose and a rather broad forehead. My black curly hair reached my waist. *It's now or never*, I thought. I smiled at my reflection, gathered all the courage I could muster and entered the building.

Inside, I was offered water in a silver chalice. Was it meant to be drunk or only admired? How could anyone afford to serve water in chalices? I was unsure what to do, so I surveyed the interiors of the building. The room was massive; the walls must have been at least fourteen feet high. As for the floor, I had never seen such gleaming marble! The wall to the left was covered with glass bookshelves that housed dozens of books, all neatly stacked. I was ushered into a room. Directly in front of me was a huge white table and a giant chair—almost like a royal throne. A golden nameplate on the table read, 'Sharmila Tejwal, PhD Philosophy'. The queen sat on her throne, her eyes focussed on the book I had written.

Only a few weeks had passed since I had first arrived in Mumbai. I had spent the early days with Veer and his family, absorbing the sights and sounds of the city. Veer had taken me to visit the radio station too. He was a famous radio jockey and his fan base was immense! It was his mesmerizing voice that had first enamoured me, lulling me into dreams of the salty ocean of Mumbai, miles away from the sweet waters of the Ganges in Rishikesh.

I had decided to spend some time in Veer's city to acclimatize myself before we got married. Very much in love, I had felt hopeful that Mumbai would embrace me and make some space for my stories on its vast canvas.

I am not a very ambitious person. But, in a fit of bravery, I had slipped in the diary in which I had written my stories underneath my packed clothes, and had made an appointment with Sharmila Tejwal. And here I was.

'Frogs hiding under wet green leaves, enjoying a drizzle...' I was suddenly brought to the present with Sharmila Ji's voice reading out loud. 'Clouds coming down to the earth, conversing with the droplets,' she continued monotonously.

I waited with bated breath as the queen shut my book and slid it across the table. Sharmila was truly a sight to behold. She was wearing a silk sari with a golden border, dark-brown lipstick and thick *kajal*. In her ears were diamond studs. Her dark hair was wound in a tight bun. Although we were indoors, she had sunglasses on. Upon close inspection the wrinkles on her cheek became visible, giving away that she was at least fifty years old.

'Meera,' she interrupted my observations, 'I granted you this appointment because I expected to see some hard-hitting stuff from a small-town writer. But you seem to be living in Cinderella's dream world!' I looked away, feeling like a scolded child. 'You have spent all your life on the broken, muddy roads of Rishikesh. And yet, you attempt to paint a picture of the oh-so-lovely scenery. Why? If you write about the reality, as opposed to narrating your fantasies, then I may be interested.'

I was speechless. This was nothing short of a thinly-veiled insult! As Sharmila stared at me through her thickly kohled eyes, I felt a strong urge to retort with something rude. Yes, any willingness to respectfully add 'Ji' after her name had now faded.

'Okay, let me guide you,' the queen declared peremptorily. 'Write about the sputum and urine in the Ganges, torn petticoats and men peeping through them, *panipuri* served in a godforsaken street cart... Write a real story curtained by lust and sin, not memories of the *rajma chawal* your mother cooked, no tales of fantasy. If you follow my advice, you may not relish the process of writing. But your readers will shower you with praise, because the dark is seductive and demonic and, most importantly, it sells. Just look at how people go crazy for Halloween.'

This was the first time in my short career as a 'writer' that anyone had spoken of literature, *rajma chawal* and *panipuri* in the same sentence. 'Literature is the language of the heart and a story must enlighten the soul,' I had heard her saying in all her interviews. Feeling duped, I sat there, expressionless, staring like a fool.

Sharmila must have mistaken my silence for aqcuiesence. 'Do you see advertisements for coffee, clothes, shoes, even books?' she asked me. 'All of them offer the temptations of the dark. Today, customers are promised *Fifty Shades of Grey*, sex with millionaires and lovemaking with vampires. Do you know what sells? Whatever happens on the bed, under the bra! I have a simple rule for this: if, while reading, you feel either disgusted or seduced, then the book is a bestseller. Do you understand what I am saying?'

Shell-shocked and humiliated, I decided to put an end to this nonsense. A fifty-year-old lady, so renowned and revered in the literary world, uttering such filth! I could not take it any longer.

'I do not want you to publish my book', I announced, standing up. I could not allow so much dirt to infiltrate my ears. I would marry Veer and build my own world, full of light and hope. My Mahadev will reside in a small temple in a corner of my heart and house, where there is no space for her favourite 'demonic dark'. Then this old, contemptuous lady will realize how mistaken she is! I may have grown up walking on the broken roads of Rishikesh, but that does not mean I cannot manifest a castle in the clouds. I am the painter of my life and nobody can dare touch my canvas.

With tremendous effort I restrained myself from voicing my thoughts. Reacting aggressively is sensible only when one is assured of an upper hand over one's opponent. I struggled to count down from ten to one to contain the fury that was simmering inside me. But that day, willpower wasn't my strong point, and my tongue slipped. 'You are wrong in assuming that people only want to read filth. They are compelled to read whatever you publish.'

'Not at all, Miss Meera Thakur,' mocked Sharmila. 'The truth is just the opposite. We sell whatever people like to buy.' She sipped from a silver chalice after she finished speaking. The golden nameplate glistened under the harsh light of the room. What a joke her educational degree was, I thought.

'Look, I run a publishing business, not a voluntary social organization,' she said rudely, pushing my book toward me. 'Books don't sell, Meera; book-asms do! Nothing sells like orgasms. And we peddle what users want to buy.'

'Now I know why your books don't reach hearts but only the area between people's legs!' I hissed, not worried about containing my reaction anymore. 'You are in a powerful position. You can bring about a revolutionary change in society if you wanted. But alas! Your sick perspective won't allow it. They say that one's vision mirrors one's perception and what you have said leaves little room for imagination as to what you are made of!'

'Please leave,' Sharmila ordered, still unusually calm. I left the building enraged, unable to believe how terribly the meeting had gone. I had no idea then that I had sown the seeds of a terrifying storm that would ravage my world one day. Perhaps my destiny had been sealed during our first encounter. Sharmila was destined to destined for victory; I was certain to perish.

※

Blue waters in front of me and the azure sky above, I found myself at the Bandra beach. I loved this part of Mumbai; it always filled me with wistfulness. I would spend hours staring at the distant horizon, watching the sea merge with the sky at twilight. This illusion of oneness would dissipate with the break of dawn, but it was beautiful while it lasted. As I touched the wet sand with my fingers, my thoughts drifted towards Veer. What if our story resembled that of the sea and the clouds? Was our togetherness also an illusion? I needed to meet Veer and know him as a person before I could marry him.

My marriage had been finalized when my mother met his at a wedding. And as soon as we consented, they set the date for March of the following year. I do not know what it was about him, but after an hour of talking I felt like I could spend my life with him.

For all the twenty-four years of my life, it had been absurdly difficult to persuade my mother to send me to Mumbai. I hadn't even crossed the city limits of Rishikesh. When I was growing up, Ma would often tell others, 'My Meera is extraordinary.' 'I don't think so, Ma,' I had told her one day when she was busily making to-do lists for my wedding. 'No extraordinary girl marries an absolute stranger just because her parents like the boy.' Ma hadn't responded. Veer's mother, on the other hand, had proved to be more understanding of my apprehensions. 'Send Meera to Mumbai for a few days,' she had persuaded Ma over the phone. 'It will help her adjust to Mumbai before the wedding.' And so, I had gone.

When I arrived in Mumbai, I was surprised at how swiftly the energy of the city had invigorated me. This was where I would manifest into reality all the stories carved on the pages of my diary. I really hoped that the heavens would bestow us with a good life here where we could live and love each other in peace.

With this newfound optimism I had proudly carried my stories into the offices of Sharmila Publications. I didn't want to become famous. All I wanted was to share my slice of paradise with the world.

That day, while sitting on the warm sand, I condemned Sharmila's viewpoint that dreams and fantasies are for the dewy-eyed and that reality is arid. I pulled out a piece of paper and a pen from my purse and began to write.

They say, 'The Dark sells because it is demonic and enchanting. It contains temptations, seductions, lust, sins and desires.'

I say, 'The Dark is not demonic and the demonic is not real. The Dark is a peaceful space which holds our dreams and the promise of a good night's sleep. The night offers us optimism disguised as dreams after the gruelling, pessimistic marathon of the day. We close our eyes and embrace the darkness in order to meditate. A mother's womb—where we begin our existence—is dark. The cosmic womb is dark. My lord Shiva resides in the deep, dark valley of Kailash, wearing dark ash; so then how can the dark be demonic or sinful?

When something happens in life
That shatters the castle of my dreams,
The skies fall upon me,
And so distant my dreams begin to seem...

The chiming of whistles,
The roar of a new beginning
Piercing the heat of the day,
The deep dark shining...
They call the dark by many names:
Ferocious, demonic, inhumane.
Yet they all allude to the same:
Dumping the garbage of their own soul in the name.
The night, the evil, the insane.
But we bury the peaceful dead in the lap of darkness.
We close our eyes to welcome sleep.
The womb is dark. Shiva is dark.
You may fear the dark,
But in the dark, I thrive.

I promise to prove that the beautiful world of my fantasy is real; in my world the light enlightens and the dark bestows peace!

A sudden gust of wind caught me by surprise. The piece of paper I was writing on blew away; I watched as it rushed toward the ocean in glee.

※

The autorickshaws in Mumbai are fascinating vehicles. They traverse the congested intestines of this giant demon of a city. Whenever I ventured out in my early days here, I was overwhelmed by the unending rush of people, the cacophony of horns, the insane rat race everyone seemed to be running. The skyline, too, was unique—against a backdrop of skyscrapers stood the desolate slums.

It was 9:30 p.m. I had been stuck in traffic for over an hour. In Rishikesh, only owls and bats ventured out at this hour.

But in Mumbai, the heady rush of vehicles showed no sign of slowing. I had no idea what had happened, but traffic had come to a standstill and people were yelling at each other from rolled-down car windows. The speakers of the autorickshaw suddenly belted out a Bhojpuri song.

> *'Do kabutar, mere do kabutar, saiyan ne uda diye,*
> *pinjare se bhaga diye, unko daba diye…'*
> *(Two pigeons, my two pigeons, my lover set them free,*
> *He released them from their cage and pressed them hard.)*

The driver was overjoyed at this late-night treat on the radio and started swaying to the rhythm. At once, I was reminded of Sharmila's words, 'Nothing sells like an orgasm.' The undisguised delight on the autorickshaw driver's face made me wonder if she had been right. Why else was such a filthy song, clearly designed to titillate, so popular?

I was lost in thought when the autorickshaw ground to a halt. I had arrived at my flat. The building I lived in had twenty-five floors, two flats facing each other on every floor. I had never seen my neighbour; the door had scarcely opened in several weeks. I jiggled the lock with my keys, holding my phone with the other hand. 'Hello, Veer. I just reached home.'

'How did the oldie like your book?'

'She found it disgusting since it didn't make her orgasm.'

'What?' the shock in Veer's voice made me grin. 'Am I talking to Meera?' he gasped. 'Are you alright? You are committing a grave sin by uttering such a dirty word!'

'I am not the one who's sinning,' I replied. 'It's Sharmila who wants literature to make her orgasm, not me. I wanted to tell her that reaching an orgasm was difficult enough at her age.'

'Never mind her,' Veer chuckled. 'You get ready quickly

and reach Joe's house. And remember, you must wear that black dress I got you.'

'Joe? Who?' I had just entered my flat and plopped down on the couch.

'Joe Khanna, Meera, my best friend. I told you about her, remember?'

'Oh, right.' Veer had indeed told me about Joe a few days ago. 'I will be there. But do I *have* to wear that black dress? You know I feel uncomfortable in such revealing clothes.'

'Can't you do it for me? If you wear that dress,' he added with a whisper, 'I can feel you with my eyes, without actually touching you.'

Sometimes Veer had a way with words. Maybe this was how he had won me over and got me to agree to the marriage proposal. I hung up and decided to get ready. Just as I was about to enter the bathroom, I heard a doorbell. It came from the neighbouring flat. Curiosity got the better of me and I rushed to the door. I wasn't a habitual keyhole-peeper, but I felt compelled to see who lived so very secretively.

A young man stood outside the flat; he must have been in his twenties and was fairly skinny. As I waited, someone opened the door very slightly. Out slipped a sallow, fleshy hand with small, round fingers, a thin wrist and fading, maroon nail polish. The boy slipped a tiny packet into the palm. The door closed and neither party could be seen or heard anymore.

The whole affair seemed clandestine and intriguing. I found myself wondering about the identity of the face behind that closed door.

Meera Meets Joe and Kalika

Jahangir Khan could have put an imposing eagle to shame. Six-feet tall with a fair complexion, he was incredibly attractive. His silky brown hair came down loosely over his forehead, highlighting his sharp, black eyes. He was about thirty-five years old and was dressed in a plain black T-shirt and blue jeans. His eyes were sharper than a camera and he was the most desirable and famous photographer in town.

'What awesome pictures!' Jahangir announced excitedly while turning his camera towards Joe. 'See how fantastic you look, Joe!'

About a foot away from Jahangir was a stage that looked like a king-size bed. It was decorated with red-velvet covers and sunflowers. Floodlights shone down on the scene from the roof of the photo studio, illuminating a naked Joe Khanna. She lay quietly on the bed, watching as Jahangir walked toward her.

'Look, your body glistens in these pictures,' he said to Joe, settling down next to her on the bed. 'I don't know about the chocolate,' Jahangir's eyes twinkled with mischief, 'but people would certainly pay to eat you up!'

Joe squirmed as Jahangir touched her breasts lightly,

apparently trying to adjust a piece of chocolate that had been placed there. The others in the studio—three men and one woman—did not even flinch. For them, a nude model was nothing out of the ordinary. As Jahangir continued to touch Joe's breasts, they pretended that the decorations needed adjustment. Jahangir would fondle her every so often, under the pretext of showing her the pictures. Joe finally snapped, 'You have placed three pieces of chocolate that you are supposed to advertise on my naked body. The viewers are sure to be confused as to what you are selling here: the chocolate or me!'

Jahangir chuckled. 'Well, how about both? The advertisements I make have a reputation to maintain. That is why I insist on selling only those products that I have sampled. Now, please excuse me while I fulfil the call of duty.' He casually picked up a slab of chocolate kept over Joe's vagina and licked it. 'Ah, sultry!' he declared.

By now, Joe was riled up. She protested, 'What is wrong with you, Jahangir? There are people around us!'

'Shush!' Jahangir stood up and shrugged. 'Shut your mouth. Mannequins do not move, my girl. Or else the world would die of shock.' Without missing a beat he ordered his assistants, 'Come on, remove the sunflowers from around Joe and spread out the roses instead. Now we shall adorn the rose with roses!'

Joe crouched on the corner of the bed as roses were placed around her. The pieces of chocolate were carefully repositioned on her body. There, the mannequin was ready for the shoot to resume.

༄

'It's the basement of *my* building, the rear seat of *my* goddamned car! You are fucking me and I cannot voice a word of protest?' Joe was breathless and drenched in sweat. 'Ouch! Go easy, Jahangir! You never do it my way.'

Joe's blue t-shirt barely covered her bosom; her red bra peeked through the edges. The windows of the car had fogged up by now because of their hot breathing and energetic movements. A few drops of sweat trickled down Jahangir's nose and fell on Joe's chest. Jahangir roughly folded her black skirt up her thighs and started rubbing himself against her legs. Joe, who was almost six-feet tall herself, struggled to get comfortable in the cramped car. Her long, straight hair had started knotting up because of the sweat. And yet, Jahangir continued to rub himself against her thighs, his hands holding Joe's neck in a slowly tightening grip. When Joe let out a sudden gasp, he smirked and asked, 'You don't like that, do you? Why didn't you invite me to your house-party tonight?'

Joe cleared her throat and replied, 'Because you are Batman. The party will be full of bright lights, and I know you are at your demonic best in the dark.' She winked and added, 'I have a thing for demons.'

Jahangir's arousal intensified and he pulled Joe closer. As he made frenetic love to her in the steamy car, Joe had no inkling of what she was losing. They crushed against each other like a stone carver's rocks; while one bloomed, the other melted.

Moments before Jahangir climaxed, Joe grabbed his butt and opened her legs wider. 'That small print shoot is not fair to me, Jazzy. I want to be the public face of 'Dark Delights'. Can you make it happen?'

'You make me come and I will make anything happen.'

Joe let Jahangir have his way with her. After all, he was the ladder to her dreams, the steps she had to climb to make for the stars. So what if she occasionally had to drown herself in the depths of darkness?

But Joe was forgetting something important. It was impossible to breathe in the deep dark, just as it was difficult breathing high up in the sky. To live and thrive, she had to walk on the earth.

※

'Dude, where is that silly girl? The party is at her house and she's missing!' Sandeep rolled his eyes at Veer. In his right hand was a huge glass of wine; his left was around Veer's shoulders.

Joe's house was overflowing with guests, like bees in a hive. Some of them were dancing to the tunes blasting from the stereo, while a few had moved to the bedroom.

'She has gone to sell chocolates today,' Veer winked at Sandeep, raising his voice to be heard above all the noise. Veer's deep blue eyes, smooth skin and curly brown hair made many girls drool over him.

'Gosh, she told you too! What a wild girl!' Sandeep settled down on a bean bag and sipped his wine. 'If she does not land this advertising campaign, she will go crazy.'

'I like to think I already am crazy,' an announcement from the doorway caught everyone's attention. There stood a dishevelled but nonetheless energetic Joe.

Veer's face lit up. He placed an arm around her waist as she slipped between the two of them, winking at Sandeep as she did so.

'So, were you two getting lonely?' she enquired, her eyelashes fluttering. 'Veer, how come your fiancé isn't here yet?'

'I deliberately asked her to arrive a little late. I wanted to gaze at you for a while, if you know what I mean,' Veer replied flirtatiously, his hand sliding up Joe's back.

'You dog!' laughed Joe, planting a kiss on Veer's left cheek. 'Thank you, baby. You never fail to make me feel special.'

'Actually,' Sandeep piped in, feeling rather left out, 'I, too, was about to lavish you with praise.'

'The opinion of second-class people does not matter. So, shut up,' Joe said.

Even though he knew she was only joking, Sandeep felt embarrassed. He looked away as Veer and Joe laughed heartily.

'Never mind her, man,' said Veer reassuringly, 'Joe and I are close friends. We were more than friends at a time, but now, since I am engaged, well… Her parties are special to me even now. Very special.'

꽃

Joe's flat was also in Bandra—a half-hour drive from my apartment in an autorickshaw. Coincidentally, she lived on the twentieth floor, just like me. For the last ten minutes, I had been standing outside, gathering my confidence to enter the party. I listened to the many noises coming from inside. I tried to listen for Veer's voice, but the music was too loud.

It didn't help that I was dressed in a green Rajasthani skirt and *kurti*. I didn't have the courage to wear the black dress that Veer had bought me. It was ridiculous! It was skin-tight and barely reached my knees. There were no sleeves and hardly any fabric on the back and shoulders. I had seen similar dresses in fashion magazines but never thought people actually wore them in real life.

I was worried that Veer would take this as a slight. After all, he had done so much to put me at ease. It was only because my parents weren't comfortable with the idea of me living with him before our marriage that he had rented an apartment for me. He must have hinted to his mother to convince mine about a trip to Mumbai. And yet, I could not even honour his innocent wish about wearing an outfit to a party.

I had stood in front of the mirror for an hour trying to make the dress more wearable. I had tried to cover the exposed cleavage and bare shoulders with a *dupatta* and a long string of beads but the outcome was laughable. Veer was a famous radio jockey with had a reputation to uphold. His friends would never stop teasing him if I showed up with such poorly matched accessories. Finally, I had opened my suitcase and decided to wear a green skirt to the party. It was from Rishikesh, and while it gave a small-town feeling, people back home thought it was quite fashionable.

Well, it wouldn't do to linger outside anymore. I cleared my throat, adjusted my hair and rang the bell. A hush spread in the room as soon as the door opened. The eerie darkness made it difficult to see the faces of the people inside. Who had opened the door?

Someone touched my right cheek. I turned hoping to see Veer. But candles lit up around me. The light illuminated cheerful faces that sang, 'Welcome to our world, Meera.' Joe came closer and kissed my cheek saying, 'Welcome, my darling.' Veer had shown me her photos before. She looked stunning—like she had just stepped out of a photograph.

Was this the world I had been so sceptical about only moments ago? I was astonished at how easily it had embraced me, making me feel like an insider within seconds. I could see Veer now; he smiled and placed a golden envelope—our wedding card—in my hands.

'Oh, Veer!' I couldn't help exclaiming, 'I can't tell you how happy and excited I am!' Veer pulled me into his arms as everyone applauded.

'Come on, guys! Let's have a kickass party for my sweetheart Veer and the beautiful Meera! Cheers, everybody!'

Joe's announcement brought me back to the present. I grew conscious of how close Veer and I were, with all those people watching us. I pulled away. Joe planted a big kiss on Veer's cheek. Veer grinned from ear to ear. If I hadn't been watching, would he have kissed her back? Joe was striking and her dress was exactly the kind Veer found attractive. I think what disturbed me most was the knowledge of the past they shared. I admired how honestly Veer had told me about their relationship before we were engaged.

I took in the party that roared around me. I had seen such things only in movies. In my town, a celebration consisted of eating *chhole-puri* cooked by my mother. If the occasion was genuinely grand, everyone went out to watch a movie at the Regal Cinema and had jalebis at the street corner. But here, all the dancing and the loud music were making me feel lightheaded. I could see some people clearly drunk, while others had already passed out on the floor.

Veer grabbed me by the waist and pulled me against his chest. His eyes looked slightly glassy; I wondered how many drinks he had downed already. 'Why did you wear this silly *ghaghra-choli* again?' he asked, staring at my breasts. 'Why didn't you wear the dress I had specially bought for you?'

'This is not a *ghaghra-choli*,' I snapped, trying to hide my discomfort. 'It is a long skirt and a kurti.'

Veer, sensing the annoyance in my voice, said gently, 'I had chosen the dress for you lovingly. I wanted you to wear it so all heads would turn toward you. Anyway, my Meera looks just as ravishing in this. Please smile now?'

How could I not feel warm inside? There was the hypnotizing voice that had made me fall head over heels for him. And now, as he whispered, his breath brushing against my ears, I nearly stopped breathing. Veer slowly stroked my back, bringing his lips closer to mine. The ground beneath my feet was slipping away. The butterflies that so many love songs promised were fluttering in my stomach. Never before had Veer and I been close enough to hear each other's heartbeat. Never before had *anyone* touched me the way he was now. I felt myself dissolving into a messy mush.

As Veer continued to kiss me passionately, as if fuelled by an avalanche of lust, my eyes sprang open. I don't know what had shaken me from my reverie. I stepped back, disentangling myself from his embrace. My breathing was uneven, and hot drops of perspiration were streaming down my neck. 'We are not married yet, Veer,' I managed to say. 'I am here only to experience your world, not lose myself in it.'

Veer, however, had no intention of letting me go. 'But this is how you will get to experience me fully, Meera,' he spoke confidently. 'If you try to know me from such a distance, your experience will be half-baked.'

'I don't care!' I forced myself to sound determined. 'I don't approve of such intimate relations before marriage. Call me old-school, but I think that a physical union can only come after the hearts become one.'

'No, my dear,' Veer disagreed, his voice mischievous. 'A physical union goes hand-in-hand with the meeting of hearts.'

'For you, maybe,' I said, flatly. 'After all, you must have become one with many women.'

Veer ignored what I said and continued to hold me tightly in his arms, but I could sense some of his passion dissipating. We belonged to entirely different worlds; our ideologies were also diametrically opposed. But from the first day we had met, we had resolved to accept each other as we were. We had vowed to create our own world, together, a quiet haven where both of us could thrive. I wonder if Veer remembered the early promises he had made to me.

The clock struck midnight, but the celebration showed no signs of slowing down. By then, the guests who hadn't yet passed out were all huddled around Joe. Several men were pretending to frisk her, laughing hysterically from time to time. Joe, who had polished off at least two bottles of liquor, was beside herself.

'Which cheap caterer have you booked?' she suddenly lashed out at Sandeep. 'The ice is finished!'

Sandeep looked flabbergasted. He opened his mouth to respond but decided against it. 'Relax, Joe,' I said trying to placate her. 'What's the big deal? I'm sure you can find ice just about anywhere. Why don't we ask the neighbours?'

'This is not Rishikesh, Meera!' she answered rudely. 'This is Mumbai!'

She weas clearly drunk. I ignored the taunt and turned to Veer. 'Take care of her, please. I will go and fetch ice.'

'But where are you going?' he demanded.

'To the flat next door, where else?'

It was well past midnight. I didn't know that I was about to turn the page to a brand-new chapter in my life. It was called Kalika Sherawat.

A girl in her teens opened the door.

'Namaste. I am Meera,' I began. 'We are having a party in that apartment and—'

The girl cut me off and snapped, 'Of course, you are having a party. The whole building knows that the people in apartment 201 become overzealous every Saturday and make it a point to suck the happiness from everyone's weekend by howling all night!'

I was taken aback. The girl was lean and short and was dressed in an ill-fitted *salwar*-suit. Her oily hair was in two plaits. Although I was not an expert, her accent didn't sound like she was from Mumbai. 'Please excuse us for disturbing you,' I apologized. I could understand her anguish. Veer had told me that Joe hosted such crazy parties every weekend, much to the chagrin her neighbours. 'I only wanted to borrow some ice. There are many guests, and we ran out.'

'Do your guests plan to drown their heads in ice until seven in the morning? Well, I cannot help you. My *Maasi* isn't home, and she strictly told me not to give any ice to anyone from that flat.'

The young girl banged the door shut. What a reputation Joe had gained! My encounter with the girl had left me with little desire to approach any of the other neighbours. I turned away from her door and was about to return to Joe's flat when I heard the door reopen. The teenager stood there with two large bowlfuls of ice in her hands. 'I figured that a neighbour must help another neighbour in times of need,' she said simply.

'Oh, thank you so much,' I smiled, wondering at her sudden change of heart. 'I will take the ice inside and return the bowls as soon as I can.'

She looked unsure. 'Is it okay if I come inside? You have so many people in there, and I don't want my bowls to get misplaced.'

It was only then I noticed how tightly she was holding the two steel bowls. 'Please come in,' I told her. 'I am sorry I did not ask you to earlier.'

'Before we go in, I must introduce myself,' said the girl shyly. 'My name is Kalika. I live here with my Maasi. Her husband works in Pune, and Maasi has gone to visit him for a few days. My parents live in Haryana. They have instructed me not to talk too much with strangers.'

I stopped myself from smiling with great difficulty. Kalika sounded so very innocent! I nodded. As we walked through Joe's door, Kalika looked around inquisitively, almost desperate to step in. The cold in her eyes a few moments ago had been replaced by curiosity.

I watched as Kalika soaked in the scene and found myself seeing things through her eyes. Her curiosity reminded me that I, too, was a stranger to this seemingly happy but asinine world of neon lights, fleeting shadows, radium masks and deafening noise. Oh, but who was I to judge? The people in this room had different lifestyles from what I was used to. It was I who sought some space in their world and not the other way round. I placed the bowls of ice on the centre table next to many empty wine bottles.

Kalika watched me from the corner of her eyes, concerned about the bowls. Every so often, a drunken partygoer would crash into her on their way to getting a refill. She would move to the left and then to the right trying to avoid people. Her eyes took in everything. I don't think she had ever seen so many intoxicated people falling over each other, such fearless displays of nudity or so much booze flowing so freely.

Kalika seemed out of place in this apartment. I was also a stranger to the glamour of this new world; the people in the room were nothing like me. But somehow, Kalika wasn't like any of us.

I have never seen the world as black or white. Although I struggled to understand many facets of the world, I believed in giving most things a chance. When tourists in Rishikesh pointed out how filthy the river had become, I managed to focus on the spiritual purity of the Ganges. Was I naïve to maintain a positive worldview and to believe in the inherent goodness of mankind? Perhaps, if my mind worked differently, Sharmila Publications might have picked up my book. I watched Kalika for a long time, my thoughts drifting to old and forgotten memories. I did not know then that on New Year's Eve, I was going to change forever. For worse.

'Hello *behenji*, why are you standing here all alone? What is your name?' A fair-skinned Sikh boy, who looked about twenty, approached Kalika. He held in his right hand a glass filled to the brim with beer.

Kalika's face paled. She took a nervous step back and replied, 'I am waiting for my bowls. If you like, I can wait outside.'

'What?' The boy grinned, fixating on Kalika's chest. 'I think you are mistaken. I can see your bowls right here in front of my eyes.'

Kalika stared at him blankly. I don't think she understood just how disgusting the boy was being.

He continued, this time stepping closer. 'By the way, I'm Sukkhi. Do you want a taste of my beer? You can sip it while you wait for your bowls.'

'Maasi has warned me not to drink any cold drinks,' she answered. 'I can drink if you warm it up.'

Sukkhi guffawed. Kalika glared at him for a moment and then looked away. She did not even look for me. Her gaze was fixed on Joe. I could see her taking in every detail of Joe's dress and make-up and the way she danced. She looked more anxious than impressed. While she was curious, she was told to stay away from Joe. But it was clear that she was fascinated by the world behind her neighbour's door and the opportunity that had presented itself was too good to pass up.

Joe held a tequila shot in her hand. She gulped it down and quickly sucked on a lemon. Veer, who stood next to Joe, did the same. Their faces went through a series of expressions—first, they grimaced as if they had just gulped down some venom; this was then followed by exhilaration, perhaps a more profound sense of stupor.

'Will you dance with me?' Sukkhi extended his hand toward Kalika, interrupting her people-watching.

'No, thank you,' she refused. 'I am fine here.'

Shrugging off her objections, Sukkhi pulled Kalika onto the dance floor. Kalika, alarmed, stood with her hands clenched tightly as Sukkhi began to enthusiastically perform bhangra steps to the beat of the jazz tunes playing on the stereo. Kalika regained her composure. She giggled at Sukkhi's desi steps and did not attempt to get away.

'Try one of these,' said Sukkhi, stopping a waiter and offering her a tequila shot. The hair on my back stood on end. I felt a strong wave of protectiveness toward the girl who had offered to help me so sweetly. I stood ready to intervene as I did not want her to be pressured into drinking.

I was about to grab Kalika's arm and pull her away. But

MEERA MEETS JOE AND KALIKA

to my utter astonishment, Kalika accepted Sukkhi's offer. She looked at Joe who was holding a similar shot glass and, as if imitating Joe, downed the shot in one quick gulp. A few minutes later, possibly due to the sheer mental pressure of the situation, she fell on the floor, apparently unconscious.

Everyone stood still. Someone turned the music off. People formed a huddle around the fainted girl on the floor.

'Who is she?' yelled Joe. 'What the fuck is she doing in my house?'

※

A pink silk curtain fluttered in the morning breeze. A giant framed photograph hung on the wall opposite Joe's bed. It was a photograph of Joe on the seashore; she was lying naked on the sand. Her hair was done up in curls that caught the sunshine and gleamed with a golden hue. Drops of water were visible on her breasts. A massive wave enveloped her bare body, appearing almost real.

How many people must have been involved in clicking and editing such a complicated picture! Kalika wondered how it was that Joe did not mind letting others see her naked. Didn't she feel any shame? Kalika shook her head, unable to comprehend this mysterious woman who slept on satin bedsheets and whose bedroom resembled a princess's. How shabby she must look in contrast! Kalika's skin was dry; her hair was frizzy. She got up from the bed carefully, afraid that her clothes would ruin the beautiful fabric of the bedsheet.

She had been at Joe's house all night. It must have been that horrible lemon drink. Her head still hurt and she had to make an effort to keep herself from falling. As she headed outside, the bright sunlight filtering through the wondows momentarily blinded her.

In the kitchen, a maid was washing up, clattering the utensils loudly. She was wearing well-ironed clothes. Her hair, which was tied up in a tight bun, had a single *chameli* flower in it. Around her neck hung a *mangalsutra* and her arms were covered in many lac bangles. Kalika got the strange feeling that she bathed in the Ganges every morning before commencing the day's work. Well, she was the maidservant of a famous model. Perhaps her employer's fashion sense had infected her to some degree.

Adjoining the kitchen was the living room—the venue for the party. It looked like a battlefield. Glasses, bottles and empty wafer packets were strewn all over. Joe sat on the couch, a thick paste all over her body. She was filing her fingernails, oblivious to Kalika's presence.

Seeing Joe in front of her, close enough to touch, made Kalika more nervous than she already was. Maasi had told her on her first night in Mumbai, 'Joe is a dangerous creature from another planet. Always keep your distance from her.' How could she disobey her Maasi so blatantly? Not only had she spent a night in Joe's flat but she was about to talk to her face-to-face.

'What is this, Didi?' the domestic worker suddenly stopped doing the dishes and walked out of the kitchen. Pointing at Kalika, she said, sounding disgusted, 'I take a day's leave and you hire a new servant? You allowed her to sleep in your bedroom as well? And I, your maid of so many years, still sleep on a mat in the kitchen! This is a terrible insult!'

Joe looked up and rolled her eyes. 'Leelavati, she lives next door. She is my neighbour.' Joe picked up her filer and resumed her manicure without batting an eye.

That's all she had to say? That servant had insulted her! Kalika was furious but managed to keep her cool. Her Maasi had told her that in Mumbai, maids were more valuable than gold. And Joe definitely needed her maid more than she did her neighbours if she was going to keep throwing the parties that she did.

Leelavati, however, refused to let it pass. 'You are trying to deny it, Didi. If she is your neighbour, what is she doing here? Have you employed her to serve alcohol at your parties?'

'Leelavati, stop bugging me so much,' Joe stopped the filing and gestured to her maid to leave the room. 'Bring us two coffees, please. Remember that mine must be black.'

The maid let out a strange, frustrated noise. 'I have told you a hundred times that my name is Laila, not Leelavati. Would you like it if I called you 'Shoe' instead of 'Joe'? Look, Didi, I must have self-respect in my life. I cannot work for someone who doesn't know my name even after I have worked for her for years.'

Kalika's eyes widened in shock. How dare a maid speak to her employer so angrily? Back in her village in Haryana, her father would scold Savita, their maid. But she wouldn't utter a single word, let alone complain.

'Okay, okay,' began Joe, trying her best to sound placating. 'Laila Rani, I promise I shall be careful from now on. Will you please bring us coffee now?'

Laila Rani obeyed. Joe patted the seat next to her. Kalika joined her on the sofa.

'You fell unconscious last night. I didn't feel comfortable sending you back to your flat since there was no one at home.' Kalika kept her eyes lowered when Joe spoke to her. Everything felt outlandish to her that morning.

'By the way,' continued Joe. 'What did you drink? How did you faint?'

'I saw you drinking *nimbu pani*, so I thought I would have some too. Was something mixed in it? I felt giddy as soon as I drank it.'

'I was drinking *nimbu pani*?' Joe looked at Kalika quizzically. 'Oh gosh, you mean a shot? So, you had neat alcohol the very first time you tasted booze? Not a very wise decision when you are all by yourself!'

'Maasi will be back in a month. I talk to my parents five times a day. You see, I am not alone.'

Kalika's defensiveness struck a chord with Joe. 'I like your optimism,' she smiled. 'Would you like some breakfast?'

Kalika shook her head. She looked up bashfully at Joe's shirt-dress that only came down to her thighs. The fabric was almost see-through. If Kalika ever welcomed a guest at home without wearing a dupatta, Kalika's father would have given her an earful. He might even have slapped her. But Joe moved around half-naked at home, regardless of whether she had company. Kalika stared at her as she walked to the bedroom and shut the door.

Laila placed two cups of coffee on the table. 'Thank you, Laila,' smiled Kalika.

Upon hearing herself being called Laila, the domestic worker smiled. 'I have made *aloo poha*,' she said enthusiastically, 'Would you like to have some?'

'Sure, thank you again, Laila. Could you please do me another favour?' Kalika pointed toward her two steel bowls, still kept on the table next to empty bottles of liquor. 'If you could wash my bowls and return them…'

'Of course, I will be right back.'

As Laila scrubbed the two bowls in the kitchen sink, Kalika knew she had won her over. Joe's rather hot-headed maid was now on her side.

The Morning after the Party

2 October 2011

The first day of October was quite a thrill. I met the arrogant Sharmila, Veer's friend Joe and Joe's neighbour Kalika at the party which had gone on into the early hours of the morning. I wondered how this morning was going for Kalika. Joe had been kind and put Kalika in her own bed.

It was seven in the morning. It was going to be another beautiful day in Mumbai. I felt a little sleep deprived, but I woke up to light a diya for Mahadev. As per my daily routine, I bathed quickly and stood with folded hands in front of my small wooden temple. I lit a *diya* before the idol of Mahadev. It was a Monday, which meant I was fasting. Many of my friends back in Rishikesh would tease me for my Monday fasts. 'You must be desperate to find a suitable groom,' they would titter. However, what they didn't know was that I was almost irrationally attached to Lord Shiva. I had worshipped him since I was a little girl. Somehow, he seemed to be after my own heart. Shiva didn't discriminate between the dawn and the dusk, the lowly and the superior. He knew that even ash could transform into gold, and gold could be burnt down into cinders.

I strung together a small lemon and a green chilli, sought Shiva's blessings and hung the assemblage outside the front door. In Rishikesh, we believed that these had the power to ward off evil. Here in Mumbai, people found beliefs like this quaint and absurd. I didn't mind their condescension, as I knew opinions could change like the wind. Scientists from other countries constantly claim that every particle in the universe possessed energy—positive as well as negative. If city-folk could accept that as truth, what was so absurd about my innocent beliefs?

As I was shutting the door, my eyes fell on the flat opposite mine. The door was, as always, shut tightly. My mother would often say, 'Only two kinds of people keep themselves behind closed doors: those who are saints and those who are prisoners.'

I had a strong yearning to meet my faceless and nameless neighbour. I wondered if Kalika had also longed for that forbidden door to open. She seemed eager to unearth the secret that lay behind her neighbour's closed door. Why is it that we always long for that which is forbidden?

I longed to meet the person who lived behind that closed door, but it was not to be. Not yet. I shut the door and walked to the kitchen to make myself some breakfast. It was going to be another ordinary day, I thought. I wish I had known then just how life-changing that morning was going to be for both Kalika and myself.

Kalika Explores the Forbidden World

The scorching summer sun burned fiercely that afternoon. Or maybe the city bus was too crowded. She adjusted her shirt; it had been a poor choice for that sweaty Mumbai day. All around her, passengers were packed against each other so tightly that it was a wonder anyone could breathe. A short, frail man caught her eye when he whistled ever so lightly. Each time the driver applied the brakes, the man brushed his hands against Kalika's thighs. Nobody else seemed to notice.

When Kalika had first arrived in Mumbai, her Maasi had spoken of the city in glowing words. 'The mischief that is so common in your small North Indian cities doesn't happen here. Mumbai is different.'

The man gave her a wink before leaving the bus at the next stop. Kalika wondered how the feeblest of men found power amidst a crowd. Like the darkness, the crowd was another faceless entity. Perhaps it was the anonymity that spoke to their baser, more predatory instincts.

Her phone buzzed in her pocket. It was Sukkhi. As much as she had disliked how he had pressured her into drinking alcohol at the party, there was something charming about having his undivided attention and so they had exchanged numbers.

'Hello,' read the message. 'I just wanted to tell you how beautiful you are.'

'Really?' Kalika smiled.

'Really,' reassured Sukkhi. 'Let's meet again? At least let me see those two bowls of yours.'

The message ended with a winking emoji. What did he mean about the bowls though? It might be quite nice to meet Sukkhi again. Back in her village, being friendly with a boy was unthinkable. But Sukkhi seemed different, debonair.

'I will come and pick you up tonight,' said another message that popped up on her screen as the bus reached its final stop.

※

It was night and an eight-seater Gypsy was speeding through the streets of Mumbai. In it was Sukkhi, accompanied by several other boys and girls. Kalika sat quietly among the strangers, watching the proceedings around her. The car stereo was set to its highest volume—it was giving her a headache. Or maybe it was the smell of marijuana that was causing her head to pound.

'What are you thinking, Miss Kalika Sherawat?' one of the girls asked her, blowing smoke into her face.

'Uh, nothing,' answered Kalika, holding her breath and wondering if turning her head away would be rude.

'You look so tense! Come on, take a puff. Otherwise Sukkhi will complain that we haven't looked after his guest properly.' The girl held out the cigarette to Kalika. A few others laughed, gesturing for her to take it.

'No, please, I am fine. I don't smoke.'

'Then there's all the more reason to begin.' The girl almost shoved the cigarette between Kalika's lips, compelling her to take a drag. The laughter around her intensified; it was punctuated only by her coughing.

'Don't worry about it, Kalika,' a boy seated next to Sukkhi gave her a one-armed hug. 'Coughing is normal on the first attempt.'

Kalika looked away, immensely embarrassed. What must everyone be thinking about her? They were a wealthy and privileged bunch—everyone was wearing designer clothes, expensive watches and elegant accessories. Sukkhi was, in fact, one of the only few who were underdressed; he had on a white vest and blue, chequered trousers. The only other underdressed passenger was a girl who wore almost the exact same combination: a white T-shirt and blue trousers.

Kalika felt a massive inferiority complex. She had searched her wardrobe for a long time to find an appropriate outfit for the night. But she had only managed to find a long red skirt, which she had paired with a blue T-shirt. In an attempt to liven up her persona, she had put on silver-plated earrings. But that had been a disastrous choice. Keeping her head low, desperate to remain hidden, she unbuckled her earrings and dropped them into her purse. Her hairy legs were hidden under the skirt.

'O Kalika *behenji*,' called out Sukkhi suddenly, 'Have you brought along your ice bowls or forgotten them at home? What shall we do when we run out of ice?' The Gypsy resounded with ear-splitting laughter. Kalika could not fathom what was so hilarious about Sukkhi's question, but she decided against saying anything. Instead, she said, 'I thought we were supposed to go to a party. Why are we driving aimlessly at this hour?' The blue-trousers girl burst into peals of laughter and was joined by most of the others. Why did these people laugh madly at everything? Was it the effect of the alcohol? Kalika couldn't begin to imagine how her father would treat her if she behaved like one of them.

'Oye Sukkhi,' said one of the boys. He had beautiful, wavy hair and was almost too skinny. 'Didn't you tell her about the kind of parties our gang organizes?'

'No problem,' announced Sukkhi. 'I will do it right now. Kalika,' he began, sending her an air-kiss, 'let me introduce you to the wildest party you will ever see!'

Kalika's heartbeat quickened. No boy had ever kissed her before, not even pretended to. The car ground to a halt on a narrow lane near Marine Lines and everyone got off. Kalika hesitated.

'Why are you sitting in there?' Sukkhi pulled her out. 'You are about to have some of the greatest fun of your life.'

Everyone huddled around the car. Sukkhi brought out an empty beer bottle and spun it on the bonnet. 'So, guys, do all of us know the rules? The bottle will decide your fate, and you will have to do whatever we ask!'

Kalika didn't have a clue. She stood and watched mutely as Sukkhi spun the bottle again. This time, it stopped in front of the skinny boy with the wavy hair. Apparently, his name was Sandy. Shouts of 'Come on, Sandy!' went up in the air; he seemed to be everyone's favourite player.

'Shut up, guys,' Sandy grimaced. 'I know you conspire to make the bottle choose me. Your sick minds enjoy watching me kiss any guy just because I'm gay!'

'Look, look,' Sukkhi interrupted him playfully. 'We won't ask you to kiss a guy this time.'

'You better not. Because, as it happens, I am hooked to one,' Sandy winked at him, linking his arm through his.

Sukkhi shrugged him off. 'Tonight, we will make you do something totally new and exciting. Come on, take off your shirt and pants!'

Excitement spread quickly through the group. Kalika's heart stopped. *Please, God, please, don't let this situation get any worse,* she thought. She covered her ears with her hands as everyone started cheering Sandy, encouraging him to get naked. Soon, before her shell-shocked eyes, Sandy took off his shirt. His pants followed suit. He stood in front of the group in tight underwear. Under the clothes, his skin appeared pink and completely devoid of hair. How was it possible for a man to be so hairless? Not a single boy back in her village had such smooth, pink skin.

Sandy caught sight of Kalika watching him keenly. 'What are you staring at, you hungry bitch? Haven't you ever seen a beautiful boy?'

Kalika immediately dropped her gaze and focussed her attention on the bottle. Sukkhi spun it again, and this time it pointed to the girl wearing the blue trousers.

Sandy let out a loud cry of excitement. 'The moment I had been waiting for!' he exclaimed. 'You enjoyed trapping me, didn't you, bitch? You always try to get me to strip down. Now it's your turn to take off your top!'

'Are you out of your mind?' the girl replied, seemingly startled. 'I am a girl!'

Was Sandy insane? Kalika couldn't believe that someone would have the audacity to ask a girl to disrobe for a silly game. A girl's modesty, she believed, was reserved for her husband. That night, however, Kalika was in the minority. The girl giggled at Sandy, took off her top in one swift motion and threw it at his face. At 3 in the morning, in the middle of nowhere, she stood wearing a black bra and blue trousers, feeling neither ashamed nor awkward. What was even more surprising was that no one other than Kalika thought it was a big deal. They were comfortable with nudity. Although she was feeling dazed, Kalika couldn't help but be rather impressed at their indifference. This was the first time that she saw a woman's naked flesh not be objectified. Was it possible that people in her small village who bundled up a woman's 'virtues' under thick clothing could learn something from the big cities?

A police siren wailed in the distance bringing the night's events to an abrupt end. Both Sandy and the girl threw on their clothes. With everyone back inside, the Gypsy whisked them away before the police car could get there.

Kalika was dumbstruck. How were these people so carefree? What if they had been caught? Her father would have dragged her back to the village and thrashed her with a cane. But the people in the car were so nonchalant. The laughter continued as if nothing at all had happened. Such raucous laughter flowed only in three situations: when one was ecstatic, deep in sorrow or indifferent to the tribulations of life. For a long time after reaching home, Kalika lay in bed wondering what was behind the laughter of Sukkhi and his friends.

※

Ten minutes had passed since the autorickshaw had dropped her off in front of the shopping mall. It was one of the largest malls in Bandra. The colossal building was covered with movie posters, advertisements and pictures of happy people. Kalika stood staring at the building, taking in the bustle of the Sunday afternoon. How strange it was that in big cities, people went to such crowded places to find solace!

When she finally stepped inside, the first store that caught her eye was one that claimed it 'sold confidence to women'. Indeed, the walls of the store were covered with portraits of beautiful, glamorous women. How could such stylish ladies not be confident? Inside, the shelves were stocked with cosmetic items of different types. Some women sat on stools in front of mirrors and busily applied powder on their cheeks. Kalika decided to talk to the receptionist.

'Is this a barber's shop, *madam ji*?' said Kalika while trying to not stare at the lady's bold, red hair.

'This is a salon, not a barber's shop,' snapped the woman, eyeing Kalika from head to toe.

'Oh, great,' smiled Kalika. 'I want to get the hair from my arms, legs and armpits removed. I want to become fair and look rich. How much will be the charges?'

'The charges for all our services are listed on this card,' the receptionist handing it to Kalika. It was in English.

'But this is in English. I know the language, but not very well. Could you please get me one printed in Hindi?'

'Sorry, we don't have one.'

'Well, could I take this home?'

'Sure, you can,' replied the woman, barely containing her laughter. Although offended, Kalika took the card and left the store. It would never do to be sensitive and take offence at such things if she wanted to change.

At the end of the row of shops was a lingerie store. The window-front displayed a white-stone mannequin wearing a shiny golden wig. The fake hair on it came down to the waist, highlighting her gold-studded panties. Kalika tried to look away, but she couldn't. The fact that someone had displayed a statue of a naked woman in a crowded mall was a giant shock to her system.

'How can I help you, madam?' a salesgirl emerged from the store. 'Do you like our display piece? It will suit you very nicely.'

Kalika was about to leave when she suddenly remembered Joe. In one of the pictures she had seen in Joe's flat, Joe had been wearing red lingerie. Kalika took two cautious steps toward the salesgirl and asked, 'Is this golden bra available in red?'

'Sure, madam,' replied the salesgirl promptly. 'It costs only two-thousand rupees. Why don't you come inside and try it?'

'What?!' exclaimed Kalika. 'You sell underwear for two-thousand rupees? Even in the biggest showroom of my hometown, this will be priced at fifty rupees. Are these bras and panties gold-plated?'

The salesgirl looked annoyed. 'Madam, this lingerie set is from Germany. It is made of superior cloth that is extremely comfortable. I am sorry, but the price is not negotiable.'

Kalika, who prided herself on being good at bargaining, seemed to have hit a dead-end here. Resigned to her fate, she tried to make amends. 'It is too expensive for me then. Could you please show me something else in red that is cheaper?'

The salesgirl rolled her eyes and motioned for Kalika to follow her into the store. She brought out a red brassiere from a drawer, and handed it to Kalika. 'Madam, this one costs one-thousand rupees. It is cheap, but I suggest you try it out. Only then will you feel the beauty of the fabric.'

'How is one-thousand "cheap"?' Kalika felt irritated with the salesgirl. 'Moreover, how can I try it out here in the middle of the store? Do you hear yourself?'

By now, the salesgirl was also agitated. But she kept calm.

'Madam,' she said softly, 'we have trial rooms for customers. You can go and try this on in there,' she pointed in the direction of a signboard that said 'Fitting Room'.

'I can't do that,' complained Kalika. 'What if someone enters the room without knocking? You shouldn't allow men to come inside your shop. It is embarrassing for the women who shop here!'

By now, many customers had lined up behind Kalika. Most of them were listening curiously. The salesgirl knew she would get scolded for holding up the line. 'Madam, this is a unisex showroom. We have garments for men too. Now, do you want to try this on or not?'

Kalika shook her head. 'No, I don't like the fabric. Could you show me something that feels softer to the touch?'

'Madam,' the salesgirl inhaled deeply. 'I implore you to try this on. It is a bestseller in our store. Look, there's a round wire below the cups and extra padding to give your chest a boost. I feel it will suit you beautifully.'

Kalika's heart beat excitedly as she glanced at the price tag once more. She hesitated before hugging the bra to her chest.

It was three in the afternoon. Kalika sat on the floor, wrapped in a pink cotton towel. Nervously, she glanced at the door—it was locked. She inspected the curtains—they were fully drawn. She now examined her naked legs and frowned at the messy hair all over. Kalika looked at the container of hot, molten wax she had placed on the side table along with waxing strips and talcum powder. Dare she do this?

Her hands shook as she picked up a blunt knife, dipped it in the container and let some wax dribble on to her toes.

Instantly, she jumped in pain. The wax was insanely hot! Her foot had turned a deep red with only a few drops. This whole affair was ridiculous. If God intended women to remove their body hair, why had he put it there in the first place?

She decided to try again. This time, she daintily applied wax around her knees, placed a waxing strip over it and then pulled it out in one swift motion. The shriek that immediately followed must have reached the heavenly courts of all Hindu deities. 'O God!' cried Kalika. 'This is how I am going to die!'

As the pain in her legs subsided, Kalika's thoughts travelled to her childhood and she cursed her father for being arrogant and lazy. What had her father done all day except for beating her? Had he worked hard and used his brains, she too might have been the daughter of a millionaire. But he was only interested in rebuking her for the tiniest mistakes.

Kalika was shocked when she saw the time—the clock said it was five in the evening. Two hours had gone by, and she hadn't got ready. Panicking, she checked her phone only to find four missed calls from Sukhhi. She threw open the cupboard. There, behind her salwar-suits on the top shelf, lay an envelope. Examining its contents, Kalika decided it was time she talked to her father.

'Bapu,' she began when her father picked up the phone. 'How are you? Yes, my studies are going well.'

Her father sounded busy, as always. 'Listen, Bapu,' pleaded Kalika. 'I wanted to ask you for some money. You send me three-thousand rupees every month but Mumbai is so expensive. It is not like Haryana. Even a cup of coffee doesn't sell for less than one hundred rupees.'

Her father flew into a rage. What was she doing in the city—drinking expensive coffee or focusing on her studies?

'No, Bapu, please don't be angry,' Kalika rushed to make amends. 'I know I can drink coffee at home. It's just that sometimes, I want to spend time with friends and wear nice clothes. The people here are different and they laugh at me if—'

Her father did not even try to understand her point of view. How foolish she had been to expect him to be generous! 'I am sorry, Bapu,' she said resignedly. 'I won't waste money on buying coffee and expensive clothes. I am hanging up now. I have to go to college.'

'Yes, I know it is evening, but we are preparing for a cultural function.'

Didn't her father hear the angst in her voice? Couldn't he ever be kind to her beyond asking her if she had learnt to cook in Maasi's absence? She didn't want a life like her mother's, sweating it out in the kitchen thanklessly. But would her life turn out differently?

It was a red-letter day. For the first time in her life Kalika wore a knee-length skirt and a sleeveless blue top. Although her outfit filled her with a new sense of vigour and confidence, she couldn't help but keep adjusting her clothes. Now and again, she arranged her hair around her shoulders, attempting futilely to cover her bare skin.

The whole concept of 'dating' was novel for her. Back in her hometown, girls and boys didn't meet alone. The most one could expect was a quick chat at a tea stall or on a shared terrace. The neighbours would interfere whenever they pleased, and any attempts at intimacy would be rudely nipped in the bud. But here in Mumbai, youngsters had so many choices. From shopping malls to coffee shops, Kalika saw couples walking hand in hand everywhere. The more time she spent in Mumbai, the more narrow-minded the people in her town seemed to appear.

'You look different today,' said Sukkhi, eyeing her bare legs with a smile. They were seated opposite each other at a café.

'Do you mean a good-different or bad-different?'

'Oh, good. Definitely good! Killer-different!'

Kalika gave him a small smile. By now, she had realized that modern women didn't beam widely. The smile had to be restrained and well-thought-out.

'What would you like to order, madam?' a waiter came to their table with a menu.

'I will have a cappuccino,' said Sukkhi. Kalika couldn't catch what he said. It sounded like *chini*, but why would anyone order just sugar?

'And what about you, madam?' said the waiter, turning toward Kalika.

'Coffee,' she replied, trying to sound casual.

'Okay, madam, but which coffee?' Why was the waiter throwing her such a doozy? What would Sukkhi be thinking about her? He probably thought she was an unsophisticated girl who knew nothing other than fainting after a single tequila-shot and embarrassing him in front of his friends. She had no idea that there could be different types of coffee.

'A cappuccino for you too?' prodded the waiter.

'Y-yes. *Kum chini* for me too.'

The waiter stared at her. Didn't he just say *kum chini*? Why then was he giving her such a disdainful look? 'Madam, there's sugar on the table. I will serve your cappuccino without sugar.'

Kalika nodded her head meekly, wishing the ground would open up and swallow her whole. She hadn't ever been so embarrassed before.

'Forget all this,' said Sukkhi after the waiter had left. 'Tell me, how is your boyfriend doing?'

'What?' Kalika trying to disengage herself from the humiliation. 'I don't have a boyfriend. Do you have a girlfriend?'

'Well, I did, but we broke up.'

'Why?'

'Because I met you.'

Kalika was overwhelmed by his response. Shyly, she said, 'It's hurtful when you break someone's heart.'

'I agree,' nodded Sukkhi. 'Which is why I never want you to break mine.'

Blushing, Kalika tried to change the subject. 'I'm sorry I was late. I had gone to a beauty parlour. It is a grand one, extremely expensive. But since my Bapu is influential, he managed to secure me an immediate appointment.'

'Beauty parlour? Why?' asked Sukkhi. 'Did you need to get a bikini wax? Don't tell me you have other plans after we finish our coffees!'

What on earth was a bikini wax? Kalika smiled faintly, pretending to understand exactly what Sukkhi meant. When he wasn't looking, she made a quick Google search on her phone. The results astounded her. Was she to believe that women in the city visited parlours to let strangers remove the hair from their private parts? As far as she knew, her mother used a razor to stay clean down there. Didn't these women die of shame? As Kalika struggled to wrap her head around this, she felt enraged with Sukkhi. How dare he make such a suggestion? All this time, she had been under the impression that it was only mannerless village boys who disrespected women. But these city-boys were no less.

Despite all this, Kalika admired the fact that the city was not fake—it did not pretend to care; it didn't push at your windows if you chose to shut them.

When the evening was slowly turning to nightfall, Kalika sat by her window and wondered about how unreal her life had become. She remembered how, back in the village, her mother laboured away from morning to night and was still disrespected by her husband. This was the life of every woman in her village. She was certain that she would never go back there. Ever since Sukkhi had dropped her off at her home after their date, she had been feeling like a fish swimming through muddy water. She did not know how deep these waters ran. She wanted to float back to the surface. However, she knew that she was no mermaid yet.

Kalika knew she had to learn to swim here in this new world. She would have to turn into a mermaid at any cost; otherwise, she would be lost in the depths. There wasn't any other option.

※

But it did not take her much time to learn the ropes. After the first few fumbling attempts, she soon knew how to breathe and swim in this gigantic tank.

'Why do we always meet in the afternoon? Let's have dinner tomorrow, no?' The boy, Vikki, clasped Kalika's hands tightly. 'Kalika, my love, you mean a lot to me.'

'Okay,' Kalika replied. 'Let's have dinner at the Taj tomorrow.'

'Great!'

'It won't be too expensive, right? The Taj is a seven-star hotel.'

'I don't care! For you, I can book a table on the moon.'

Kalika giggled. Today, her skirt didn't even reach her knees. Her blue top fit her torso rather too tightly. Vikki, whom she had seen at Joe's party and later befriended at Sukhhi's house, smiled back indulgently.

Only a few days had passed since her first encounter with Joe, but Kalika had already mastered many new life lessons. Now, she was an expert not only on the different kinds of coffee and waxing but also well-versed with the ways of boys.

※

'Why do you like wearing maroon so much?' One of the girls, Simmi, from her girl gang was scrutinizing Kalika's T-shirt. 'Don't you know that black is in vogue these days.'?

'Really?' Kalika sipped from her teacup. 'Listen, I wanted to tell you something.'

'What?'

'I met your friend Vikki recently. He asked me to have dinner with him at the Taj.' Kalika tried to hide the note of pride in her voice but failed.

'Who? That spoilt rich kid?' Simmi didn't look impressed. 'He will spend five-thousand rupees on the dinner and fuck you later to recover his money. Anyhow, you will have a fun night, free of cost!'

Kalika scowled, pretending to shrug off the subject. 'I better leave. I'm meeting Shyam at his place in some time.'

'Why are you meeting Shyam? Where the hell did you meet him?' Simmi asked, surprised. 'He is completely broke. You're wasting your time with him.'

'I met him at Sukkhi's house. He's Sukkhi's friend. And by the way, I don't befriend people only for their money,' said

Kalika, sounding offended. 'Shyam seems quite nice.'

'You poor girl! All these boys are the same; not one is interested in your heart!'

'You seem to be speaking from experience.'

'I am,' she said. Simmi finished her tea and bit into a *pakoda*. 'I had a boyfriend who I thought loved me with all his heart. And one fine day, he abandoned me, never to be seen or heard from again.'

'Well, there's no harm in giving Shyam a chance, is there?' said Kalika as she picked up her purse and walked out of the restaurant.

※

'Will you be my girl?' Shyam asked as he planted a clumsy kiss behind her ears and tried to embrace her. Kalika thought that all these boys were indeed just the same. She smiled at Shyam and replied, 'That depends. Will you take me shopping?'

'Anything for you!'

Really, this was getting too easy. Kalika, dressed in a mini skirt and a translucent yellow top, almost hugged herself with delight. She had applied a dash of glitter on her cleavage. Getting boys to do her bidding was a cakewalk by now.

※

'You are becoming quite a pro at this, I must say,' Simmi congratulated Kalika when she told him about her shopping date with Shyam.

'It wasn't difficult,' she blushed. 'Boys keep their brains tucked between their legs.'

Simmi giggled. 'You may be right, you know. Listen,' she added importantly, 'we have to do something major now. You must get a new name.'

'What? Why?' Kalika asked defensively.

'Well, Kalika is an ancient, outdated name. It doesn't go with your new personality. The first time you joined our gang—that night when we were hanging out in the car—I wanted to tell you this.'

'Okay,' she agreed half-heartedly. 'It was my father who gifted me this unfortunate name. But how will you find me a new name?'

'Kalika darling, from fucking to riding a horse, whatever you need to know, Google Uncle is here to help. Let me search for your new identity.' Simmi tapped away on her phone screen. 'Now, we're onto something. How about Kelly? Or Kitty?'

'I like Kitty!' smiled Kalika. 'It has a nice ring to it.'

'Great! Come on, let us light a cigarette to celebrate your christening.' Simmi brought out a packet of cigarettes from under the pillow and offered one to Kalika.

She looked on, dismayed. 'I don't know how to smoke.'

'There's nothing to know,' Simmi brushed off her hesitation. 'Smoking is easier than fucking.' She demonstrated by lighting her cigarette, taking a deep puff and blowing the smoke at Kalika's face.

'People have lost all civic sense! Who rings the bell so loudly at two in the afternoon?' Laila opened the door to Joe's apartment, ready to rebuke whoever had come to visit. It was Kalika.

'Leelavati, is Didi home?' Kalika stood outside impatiently, trying to look over Laila's shoulders.

'Who are you?' Laila fumed as she heard the word 'Leelavati'.

Kalika was astonished. She had been certain that Laila had warmed toward her when they had met. 'Have you forgotten me? I am Kitty, um, Kalika, your neighbour.'

'You may be *kutti* or *kamini*, what do I care? Get out of here!'

Kalika realized mistake. She hastened to placate Laila her mistake. She hastened to placate Laila who, after taking care of Joe for so many years, had become quite obnoxious. 'I am sorry, Laila. I forgot your name. Please let me come in. I must see Joe Didi.'

Laila smiled. 'Okay, come in. I will make some tea for you and you can wait until madam arrives.'

Kalika plopped down on the comfortable couch and picked up a magazine from the centre table. It was a glossy fashion magazine and there, on the front page, was Joe. The picture made Kalika restless. She got up and walked to Joe's bedroom. Her eyes fell on a blue paper bag on the bed. Unable to contain her curiosity, she peeked at the contents. Inside was a gorgeous sari, beautifully embroidered and glistening in the afternoon sunlight. The price tag was still intact. It said ₹1,00,000.

There had to be a mistake. How could a sari cost one lakh rupees? In Haryana, her father managed an entire year's groceries in that amount! Only a few days had passed since she had made an unsuccessful attempt at upping her monthly allowance by two-thousand rupees. Joe, on the other hand, was swimming in money!

Kalika opened Joe's wardrobe. It was lined up with exquisite dresses. She felt the fabric of a few and couldn't believe how soft they were. In the corner of the top shelf, partially hidden under a scarf, was something that next captured Kalika's attention: a red bra. The cups were stuffed with cotton to provide a sexy lift and an aluminium wire held them in place. The bra looked like the one she had seen at the mall some time ago but hadn't been able to afford.

She felt an irrepressible urge to try on the bra. But did she dare? Kalika hurriedly glanced at the kitchen; Laila was still preparing tea. Now was her chance. Without second-guessing herself or giving her thoughts any time to breathe, she threw on the bra. It fit her like a dream. She admired herself in the mirror, pursing up her lips like the models she had seen in magazines.

'I look even sexier than Joe *Didi*,' she said out loud. Her bra, which cost much less, lay bunched up on the floor. 'There is bound to be a difference,' Kalika told her reflection. 'In a bra that costs a fraction of this one, I look like a girl from a lowly family. But now, just see what a hot babe I have become!'

Kalika was blushing so much her cheeks had turned red. She had let loose her hair and it hung over her shoulders. Her tight blue jeans complemented her narrow waist.

She was thinking about how much the red colour suited her complexion when a loud clattering startled her. It was Laila, staring open-mouthed at Kalika. The teacup was in pieces on the floor. The tea had spilt onto an expensive-looking floor rug that Joe had placed outside her bedroom door. Kalika felt certain that she was in for some major scolding. Instead, Laila began blabbering, '*Hai Raam*! Now I know how madam's breasts always look so big! I used to think these high-society women walked about with cabbages stuffed into their chests!' Laila was clearly exhilarated at her discovery.

Kalika froze. Laila stared at her unabashedly, like a dog drooling at the sight of a chicken bone. Disturbed, Kalika scrambled to cover her breasts with her hands and tried to speak with composure. 'Laila, pick up the teacup and prepare some fresh tea for me. Leave the room right now.'

It seemed Laila hadn't heard. Kalika turned away, rushing to pick up her clothes from the floor. Suddenly, Laila, unable to control her excitement, ran up to her and grabbed the bra cups with both hands. 'Leelavati!' screamed Kalika, pushing her away. She was shocked. 'What's wrong with you? Have you lost your mind? You can't just grope me!'

This snapped Laila out of her haze. She realized, to her horror, that in the excitement of her discovery, she had ended up groping Kalika. 'Don't you dare insult me!' she hissed, trying to turn Kalika's attention away from her own crazy behaviour. 'My name is Laila, as you very well know. And don't you have any shame? Hmm? Why are you wearing madam's clothes without her permission? I will tell her everything as soon as she's home!'

Kalika tried her best to ignore the threat. She was having trouble digesting what had just happened. Unable to react, she stood dumbfounded and watched Laila walk out of the room.

※

It was twilight, and the room was dimly lit. Joe was sitting on the couch with a glass of wine in her hand. On the table in front of her was a half-empty bottle of wine and her phone. An onlooker might have been alarmed at the speed with which she switched the channels on her television. She was trying to not reach for her phone. Finally, failing to restrain herself, she picked it up and speed-dialled a number. 'Where are you, Jahangir? Why have you been dodging my calls for the last ten days?'

Joe pressed the phone to her ear like a crazed woman

whose life depended on it.

'H-hello? Jahangir! Please don't disconnect the call. Why didn't you choose me for the shoot? How could you just give the project to that Australian model? You had promised it to me! You cheat!' Joe screamed but Jahangir had already hung up.

Darkness had descended, and it filled Joe's soul. She gulped down another glass of wine and flicked through the television channels. She must have dozed off for a while because when her eyes opened, Kalika was sitting beside her.

'What's wrong with me,' Joe murmured under her breath. 'I forgot to close the door. Such a forgetful drunkard I have become.'

'It's okay, Didi,' said Kalika reassuringly. 'I had come to see you a few days ago. Laila must have told you? I just wanted to tell you that whatever she said about me is a lie. Nothing like that happened.'

'What will you drink?' slurred Joe completely ignoring what Kalika had just said. *Had Laila not told Joe anything or was Joe too drunk to remember*, wondered Kalika. 'Have some wine,' she said, pushing the bottle toward her. Kalika poured herself a glass and gulped it down like she would a glass of cold lassi.

'Easy, easy, my girl,' Joe patted her on the back, alarmed at her speed of drinking. 'You don't gulp down wine in one go.'

'Don't worry, Didi,' replied Kalika, all matter of fact. 'I've been drinking since my childhood. I know all there is to know about alcohol.'

'Really? Since your childhood?' laughed Joe. Something about Kalika reminded Joe of her younger self. She might have said something similar many years ago, when she had been trying to fit into the world of glamour. People laughed at anyone who stood out or failed to fit in. 'So, you have grown up now?'

Kalika felt awkward. Growing bored of the conversation, Joe turned away and stared at the television again. Kalika stared at Joe's beautifully painted nails, her broad shoulders and slender neck. With her flowing hair and the glass of wine held stylishly in one hand, Joe looked a lot like Menaka, the angel who had managed to seduce even the most focussed yogis.

The television anchor was speaking in a cheerful voice. 'Good evening, friends! Welcome to your favourite show: *Bollywood Ki Baatein*. Today's breaking news: a foreign woman has taken Bollywood by storm! Hunny Jasmine—the ruling superstar of the adult entertainment industry—has been offered a contract of three crores for a movie.'

Kalika heard the television remote fall. Then, she almost jumped out of her skin when Joe let out a piercing scream.

'She gets that kind of money for stripping off her clothes! And if she chooses to wear them, she will get paid even more by those asinine fashion brands and movie producers!' Joe was talking to herself, oblivious to Kalika's presence in the room. 'What about those who have been struggling for years, believing that hard work brings success? "Adult entertainment industry", my foot! She is nothing more than a prostitute!'

Kalika was dumbstruck. She couldn't believe that the confident, composed Joe had tears streaming down her cheeks. Nervously, she gulped down the remaining wine, dribbling a little on the carpet. Joe stopped sobbing and stared at the fallen drops of wine. Kalika was unsure how to react. She was also afraid that Joe would resume her screaming at any moment. Quietly, she fled from the apartment.

It was past midnight. Rhythmic English music blared over the speakers in Kalika's apartment. She stood in front of the mirror wearing pyjamas, an empty glass in one hand and a pen in the other. She looked exactly like Joe, didn't she? Trying to act casual, Kalika imagined that the pen was a cigarette and pretended to take a puff. Then, she sipped from the empty glass. Maybe the air in her apartment was magical that night or her mind was playing tricks on her, but she caught a twinkle in her eyes. She held her head high up and fluttered her eyelashes. Ah, she looked like the very epitome of confidence!

Kalika rarely stayed up so late, but that night she didn't feel at all sleepy. She opened her laptop and logged on to the internet. In the search bar she typed in 'Joe'. Many results popped up, but they were not what she was looking for. She tried to recall the name of that actress whom Joe had angrily called a prostitute. Ah, yes! 'Hunny'. As the search results loaded, a shiver went down her spine as if she had unearthed a secret not many knew.

What popped up on her laptop that night left a permanent mark on her heart. Hunny Jasmine, it seemed, had been a prostitute in several countries. She was in India now and had bagged a major movie contract. She didn't seem to have any acting skills whatsoever, or so the news reports claimed. But the truth was bare for everyone to see: she was swimming in money.

Kalika was convinced that everything she had learnt so far in life was a mirage. It was too bookish and out-of-date to believe that hard work or aptitude held the keys to success. Joe, whom Kalika had thought to be successful, was a testament to this. Joe's rant was still fresh in her mind, 'She gets that kind of money for stripping off her clothes! And if she chooses to wear them, she will get paid even more...'

Really, what nonsense her textbooks had taught her all

her life. 'With our heads held high, we aim for the skies. We crush the earth under our feet and hold the skies in reverence,' her teacher used to say. 'But we must remember that even the birds have to return to the earth for food and shelter. It is the earth that keeps us grounded.' Kalika was mulling over the futility of this advice when she heard murmurs coming from outside. She rushed to her door and opened it a little.

There in the corridor stood Joe, pressed against the wall. A man was forcibly pushing himself against her, ignoring her cries of protest. Kalika recognized the man; he was the renowned fashion photographer Jahangir Khan whose picture she had seen in Joe's magazines.

Was Joe annoyed by Jahangir's advances? Should she venture out to help her? Kalika decided against it: Joe's eyes had the unmistakable look of passion. She stood silently behind her door, unable to draw her eyes away from the scene. Jahangir, who looked inebriated, was now sucking at Joe's lower lip. He slipped his right hand under her T-shirt and, with his other hand, pinched her buttocks. The erotic tussle had glued Kalika to the spot. She stood transfixed long after the duo had gone inside the apartment.

Kalika's breathing was uneven; her lips were parched. What had she just seen? Her mother hadn't even let her watch lovemaking scenes in movies, but here was real life, more passionate and overwhelming than she had pictured. When she sat down on the sofa, her hands seemed to develop a mind of their own. She slipped her left hand under her light-blue nightshirt. The other hand went under her pyjamas, gently stroking the skin between her thighs. Kalika rested her head against the back of the sofa and closed her eyes. Even with her eyes closed, she couldn't stop herself from picturing Joe and

Jahangir over and over again, caught in a tight embrace, their lips melting against each other's, their bodies moving in sync. As Kalika tightly clasped her breasts, her breathing grew more uneven, and she let herself lose all sense of time and place.

Suddenly, an old, long-suppressed memory entered her mind. The door to her apartment in Mumbai transformed into a rusty green gate. Kalika found herself gazing at an open verandah covered with a thick layer of sand. She was back in her hometown. She saw her father sitting on a cot and her mother standing near him. Both of them were staring at her in anger.

In a flash, Kalika's father reached out and roughly pulled her ear. Smack! A resounding slap on the cheek followed. Kalika's face burned in pain and humiliation. Her father shouted, 'Why did you step out of the house without your dupatta? How many times have I told you that a family's honour rests in its daughter?'

Her mother added, 'Let's send her to my sister in Mumbai. She will set her straight. As soon as she completes her graduation, we will get her married. Only then will we be able to breathe in relief!' Angrily pulling at Kalika's hair she went on, 'It's because of girls like you that people detest the birth of a daughter. Boys create no such problems. Their parents don't lose sleep as we do over you, you insensitive girl!'

Kalika had wanted nothing more than to leave that house. And today, in Mumbai, as she sat touching herself for the first time in her life, she wanted those painful memories to leave her forever. She started stroking herself harder, compelling her body to transcend the horizon and break free. She was soaking wet by now; sweat flowed down her brows. Suddenly, she felt tears flowing down her cheeks. *Why is this happening now*? she wondered.

Exasperated, Kalika sat up and opened her eyes. She picked up a flower vase from the table and flung it. The pieces lay shattered on the mosaic floor, much like Kalika's futile attempts at liberation. It wasn't easy to soar in the skies. Perhaps, that was why so many people spat on the surface of the earth. To express their rage.

Beyond Her Wildest Dreams

25 December 2011

Nearly three months had passed since I had entered Veer's world in Mumbai. The perpetual commotion, the wine, the superficial crowd, the English music that constantly blared in Joe's apartment remained incomprehensible but had become more familiar. I had met Joe very briefly at my welcome party. I remember how resplendent she had looked.

Now, Joe was throwing a Christmas party and Veer had dragged me to it. I had worn a long black cotton skirt embroidered with golden flowers. The sleeves of my kurta were buttoned at the wrist. I accessorized with silver bangles that clinked when I moved. 'You look nice,' Veer had said to me earlier that evening, struggling to sound sincere. Once again, Joe, with her skin-tight, low-cut gown, looked beautiful. I knew that Veer would prefer that I dressed like Joe.

'What's the matter, Veer?' Joe clicked her glass against his and raised her eyebrows. 'Why aren't you drunk yet? Is this your first drink?' She feigned a cry of shock.

'I'm sober because you are too covered up in this gown,'

replied Veer, kissing Joe on her right cheek. 'I'm not a fan of anything that hides you!'

Joe giggled; Veer winked. How could they continue this banter in front of me? Was I invisible or just inconsequential?

Well, nothing escaped me. As I struggled with these thoughts, a vaguely familiar girl approached me.

'Hello, Didi,' she smiled at me. Dressed in a short red dress that barely reached her knees, the girl was quite stunning. 'You look pretty,' she complimented me. 'Do you remember me? I am Kalika, the girl from whom you borrowed ice.'

It couldn't be! So, that was where I remembered her from! But the girl in front of me was light years away from the shy, geeky person I had met many nights ago. 'I am well,' I managed to say. 'How are you doing, Kalika?'

'Please call me Kitty,' she cut me short. 'I have changed my name. Isn't it classy?'

I hesitated. I might have visibly flinched. All those nights ago, this girl had been so shy and hesitant. How the tables had turned!

'What would you like to drink, Meera Didi?' she continued cheerily. 'Whisky? Wine? I'm drinking wine. It's one that Joe Didi loves.'

Something about the way she referred to Joe bothered me a little. She was obviously imitating Joe in an attempt to gloss over a past that was too humiliating. I felt that Kitty was a persona she had created to trick the world as well as herself. I had always felt like a loner in Veer's world. But here was someone as lonely as me. Kalika, too, was trying to blend in.

'I don't drink, little girl,' I said emphatically, but I don't think she caught the note of disapproval in my voice.

'Oh,' said Kalika, disappointed. 'That's boring. Anyway, I

hope you enjoy the party, Meera Didi. I am going to go greet the other guests.'

Some nights ago, this girl didn't even have the courage to walk through Joe's door. But today she was socializing like it was second nature to her. I wondered how people were drawn to the allure of darkness. Was it the transparency of light that made things uninteresting? And, by virtue of that, was what lay in the darkness made more desirable because it was unknown?

I felt unsettled for a long time that night. Was Kalika's transformation part of her own idea of life or was it taken from the people she met? Did she want to be happy or accepted?

It was 3 a.m. My head was pounding. All I wanted to do was to go home and sleep. But the party was on and Veer would stay until everyone had passed out of exhaustion.

I saw Kalika peering into a giant mirror, all glassy eyed. It was clear that she had consumed more alcohol than her frail body could handle. I darted across the room in time to prevent her falling to the floor.

'Oh, thank you, Meera Didi,' Kalika began, clutching my arms. 'You know Sukkhi, don't you? He forced me to drink again.'

'Let's go home, Kalika,' I said firmly, trying to pull her away.

'My name is Kitty. I have told you before.'

Even though she was drunk and had little control over her own body, her resolve to assume a new identity in this new world was as strong as ever. I didn't respond and made another attempt to lead her to the door.

'Not like this, not like that!' She suddenly started mumbling, at no one in particular. 'Don't do this, don't do that! Don't drink, they say. Bapu sits in that cot and drinks like a fish every evening! Are the rules different for men and women?'

'No,' I sighed.

'Are only boys allowed to dream? Can't girls dream too?'

'Of course, they can.'

Kalika wasn't even listening to my responses. She was overrun by her memories and emotions. I held her tightly as we walked to her apartment. She was still quite disturbed when I led her to the bed, but soon, she was fast asleep.

I didn't feel like going back to the party. It was noisy and made me anxious. I sent Veer a text and took an autorickshaw home.

I got home when the morning sun was peeking over the horizon. Kalika was probably in a deep slumber, but I was wide awake. My thoughts kept wandering to her questions. Her desperation for freedom, to fit in, to fly, the desire to rebel against what was normally preached to girls... When I had asked for ice that night, Kalika had rushed to shut the door. But it seemed that Kitty was willing to open any door that would lead to freedom.

Perhaps, if I hadn't invited Kalika into Joe's world that night, Kitty would never have been born. But then again, who was I to say that Kalika would have been better off had she not morphed into Kitty? As I tossed and turned in bed, I couldn't stop feeling guilty. Would anything have changed if I had let her stay behind the closed doors of her flat? Damnation was about to befall us, and I was the one to blame.

Meera Meets Maheen

2 October 2011

While Kalika was waking from her first hangover and shaking hands with Joe, I finally met my mysterious neighbour.

The morning we met was ordinary in every other way, and we could never have known how significant that meeting would be. As per usual, I stepped out to hang a lemon and chilli by a string from the doorframe of my flat. Perhaps the ritual truly brought some magic that day as my neighbour emerged from behind her door and shook hands with me.

She was slightly plump and had thick black hair that reached her thighs. She was about five feet tall and must have been a couple of years younger than me. Her white salwar-suit was embroidered on the edges. It had been paired with a golden stole which was neatly adjusted around her chest. But it was her make-up that truly stood out. I had never seen anyone slather on so much of it! I, who had virtually no experience with make-up, could see the clumsiness of her grooming. The contrast between the colours on her face and those on her brown neck were ludicrous.

'Salaam. I am Maheen Khan,' she said softly. I was so excited about meeting her that I forgot to reply.

'You live in this flat, don't you?' she prodded when I didn't say anything.

'You noticed?' I finally blurted.

'Yes, I noticed,' she asserted simply with a smile. 'After all, I live right in front of you.'

How blunt I must have sounded! I started again, 'No, I meant only that you don't usually come out of your house... But it's good to meet you, Maheen.'

She observed me silently for a while. 'You are right,' she nodded, 'I live right opposite you, but we have never interacted with each other. This was my mistake. Neighbours should look out for each other.'

'Don't worry about it,' I rushed. There was something innocent about her voice that struck a chord with me.

'And yet, today, you are conversing with me so politely,' she continued. 'I feel so selfish that I have sought you out after all these weeks only to ask a favour.'

'I would be happy to help.'

'Well,' she said hesitantly, 'I have to do some shopping, but I have no one to accompany me.'

'I would love to come with you,' I said.

Maheen's eyes twinkled at my response. A smile lit up her face and seemed to shed years from her age. Underneath her thick make-up, there seemed to lurk a teenage girl who secretly enjoyed playing with her toys.

'But before we head out,' I returned her happy smile, 'I think you should know the name of your companion.' Holding Maheen's hands in mine, I said, 'I am Meera.' She smiled and tapped her forehead, apologizing for not asking me my name. It was the first time in Mumbai that I had felt such a warm connection with a stranger.

※

It was a windy afternoon. The autorickshaw zipped through traffic toward the shopping mall. A gust of wind caught us unaware. Maheen's burqa and white salwar fluttered wildly, almost as if eager to break free. She quickly rearranged the burqa, ensuring that only her eyes were visible to the world.

'How are you finding Mumbai?' she turned to face me. 'I know you haven't been here long; I saw you the day you arrived.'

'It is a lot different from my hometown, Rishikesh,' I replied, amused that Maheen, like me, had also been keeping tabs on me from behind her closed door.

'I can understand,' she nodded. 'You know, I am from Habibganj. It is a small but lovely town in Bhopal. I moved here a year and a half ago—after I got married. My parents and three sisters still live in Habibganj.'

'Wow, you have three sisters? Are they married?'

'No, my parents are looking for suitable grooms. They want a man like my husband, but that isn't easy. Back home, everyone talks about how fortunate I am to marry a good man and live in a big house in the city. My husband fulfils all my needs. Do you know he recently got a giant television for me? He knows I am a couch potato.'

Maheen spoke for fifteen minutes; I had been listening patiently. It was nice to hear her talk and not be expected to share much about myself. But Maheen seemed to realize that she had been monopolizing the conversation. 'What a chatterbox I am!' she shook her head. 'We have almost reached the mall and I haven't asked a single thing about you.'

'That's all right,' I said.

'Anyhow, I already know all about you.'

'Really?'

'Yes! The man who comes to meet you often is your husband. He possibly has a career in shipping, which is why he can only visit at intervals. Isn't that right?'

The thought of Veer working in shipping made me giggle. 'Um, you are probably referring to Veer. He is my fiancé; we aren't married yet.' I could sense Maheen was rather startled and decided to elaborate.

'I am from Rishikesh, remember? My aunt is a friend of Veer's mother. She had helped my mother and Veer's mother arrange our marriage. But before getting married, I wanted to understand Veer's world. So, my mother decided to send me here for a while.'

'That's brilliant! Your *Ammi* made a terrific decision. If you hadn't come here, how would we have met?' Maheen's eyes sparkled with delight. 'Tell me, Meera, what does your fiancé do?'

'He is a radio jockey.'

'What a coincidence!' Maheen exclaimed, clasping my hands excitedly. 'My brother is also an expert at repairing radios and televisions. Your fiancé and my brother are in the same trade.'

Maheen looked so pleased that I decided not to correct her. On that first afternoon we spent together, Veer assumed the role of a radio-repairman.

In the past few years, many shopping malls had sprung up in Bandra. We entered one of the more famous ones. I noticed Maheen clutch her purse tighter. She looked around with a curious mix of excitement and trepidation. She did not seem like she frequented shopping malls.

As we walked, Maheen stopped in front of a lingerie store. I could see it in her eyes: she wanted to go in but was feeling self-conscious. I thought that I would encourage her a little. 'Let's go inside,' I said, taking her arm.

'No, no!' she said and shook herself free. 'Can you please buy one for me from this store? I will stand here and wait for you.'

'Don't be silly. I don't know your size or your taste. Why don't we go in and look around?'

'Please understand,' she lowered her voice. 'There are no female employees in there.' Visibly uncomfortable, she went on, 'How can I talk about bras with strange men?'

I didn't know how to respond to this logic. So, I decided to side-step it and encourage her once more. 'Maheen, do come in. I don't know your size…'

'Can't you make a guess?' Maheen implored. 'I trust your judgment.'

Shaking my head, I decided to give it a shot. I observed Maheen. She appeared to be rather flat-chested under her loose burqa. It was difficult to gauge what she looked like because it seemed large enough to fit two more people under it. How did Maheen not find it bizarre? Or wait, was it an intentional effort to hide her curves?

The constant societal judgment on women's clothes always got on my nerves. Why were loose, long clothes considered virtuous but well-fitting and short ones slutty? When I saw Joe wearing her tight dresses, I was disturbed not by the length of her skirts but by people's reactions to them—particularly Veer's flirtatious advances. Veer was a typical man. I saw him sneaking glances at Joe's cleavage on the pretext of admiring her clothes.

It might have also been how differently Maheen and I were brought up. We both hailed from small towns but this did not mean that I had let my thoughts about clothes become linked to virtues.

I wondered if Maheen dressed so conservatively out of choice, for religious reasons or if she was ashamed of her body. In Rishikesh, one of my teachers would tell us the story of a lion cub that was separated from his family and grew up with sheep. The cub learned the ways of sheep. Then, one day, when a ferocious lion attacked, the cub, too, ran for his life. He did not know who he was and knew nothing of the strength he posessed. Maheen, like the little cub, had been trained to think of herself as undesirable. Her perspective towards life and her choices were a result this upbringing.

I glanced back. She stood at the entrance to the store, looking around nervously. Inside, I picked up a black padded bra that seemed to be her size and held it up. She shook her head, mortified. I repeated the ritual with four more bras, feeling more awkward each time. The manager had been watching us, clearly amused. Finally, Maheen approved a maroon bra. I heaved a sigh of relief, got it billed for her and left the store.

After the embarrassment at the store, things began looking up. Maheen proceeded to shop like a champ. She started with a knee-length frock and then went on to buy different shades of nail polish, lipstick and foundation—she was on a roll. She also bought several tubes of fairness creams which explained why the colour of her face looked so different from that of her neck. I accompanied her from store to store, my curiosity and confusion deepening. I wondered when and how she would use all these products. She remained covered by a burqa all the time!

When ready to leave, Maheen stopped in front of a photo studio near the exit. She pulled me inside. 'Please give us two prints,' she instructed the photographer, as she dragged me in front of the camera. 'I will keep one and you can keep the other, Meera,' she said smiling.

I didn't know how to react. I smiled at the camera awkwardly, standing next to a woman covered from head to toe, barring the eyes. Other than the two of us, no one would know that it was Maheen. But the photograph served a different purpose for her: it was a reminder of our afternoon together.

'Do you like being photographed?' I couldn't help asking Maheen while leaving the photo studio.

'I love it. In fact, that's partly why my Ammi and *Abbu* married me to my husband. He takes photos for a living. I like how photos feel to the touch; you cannot get that with mobile phones.' She looked at me and added, 'I hope you will keep this photograph as a token of our friendship.'

Several hours had passed since we had begun our shopping trip, but Maheen seemed reluctant to return home. We went to the beach where we sat quietly side by side on the sand. We watched the sunset and admired the glorious tangerine skies. Every so often, she examined her shopping haul excitedly, sorting through the items. A short distance away, a hawker was selling panipuri to a small group of women. One of them was struggling to enjoy the panipuri without getting any on her hijab. If Muslim men had to go through this, they would alter their holy book in an instant.

'This frock is beautiful, but he overcharged us,' said Maheen pulling my attention away from the panipuri stall.

'What?' I asked her absent-mindedly.

Maheen didn't mind that I was distracted and went on, 'You must be wondering why I purchased all these things. Well, they aren't for me. I bought all this for a friend of mine who lives in Habibganj. In our small town, we don't get such modern, imported cosmetics and dresses.'

She couldn't meet my eyes and busied herself with a shopping bag. It was clear that she rarely lied; this was perhaps one of her first lies in ages. I didn't know for whom she did all this shopping but it was not for any friend.

The crowd on the beach had begun to thin. We were among the last ones left. Maheen's burqa was fluttering in the sea breeze, but she was not as bothered by it as she was in the autorickshaw. Now that it was evening, she didn't seem as shy. I could see that underneath her black burqa, she was wearing a white suit embroidered with red flowers. Coincidentally, I was also dressed in white.

Maheen saw me staring at her clothes. 'You look lovely in that salwar suit, Meera,' she smiled. Turning away from me, she continued. 'You know, white is my favourite colour. I like black the least.'

I gazed at Maheen's happy face; her eyes were smiling up at the twinkling sky. 'Maheen,' I encouraged, 'nobody is around now. You can remove the hijab if you want to.'

Unexpectedly, she did. She grinned at me and gave me a surprising compliment, 'How beautiful you are, Meera! So fair too! Your fiancé is very fortunate.' The moment transported me to several months ago when I had first set foot in Mumbai. 'I am fortunate to have you,' Veer had told me, giving me a one-armed hug. Our marriage was in the cards; the date glittered before my eyes like a dream.

I remembered the time when Sharmila had trashed my stories. I had come to this very seashore to vent about it. What was it about the sea that made people open up? Was Maheen pouring her heart out to the roaring waves? Was she having a conversation with the ocean to which I wasn't privy?

'Allah! It is nearly seven! We must go,' said Maheen, standing up with a start.

Before I could say anything, Maheen's phone started ringing and her face lost its radiance. The screen displayed '*Shauhar ji* Calling'. Frantically accepting the call, Maheen blabbered, 'Hello ji, I will be home in ten minutes. I am just around the corner with the lady who lives opposite us. Hello... Hello?' I could sense that she had deliberately disconnected the call. Turning to me, she spoke with a considerable effort to appear calm. 'My husband is quite protective of me since I am not acquainted with the city yet.'

Our journey back home was quick and quiet. Maheen's black burqa covered her white outfit carefully again.

༜

Dumping the shopping bags on the bed, Maheen pressed the phone to her ears. 'No, no... I reached home long ago. Yes, just five minutes after your call.' She sat down on the floor and asked her husband who was on the other end of the line, 'Are you coming home? Listen ji, I have cooked your favourite dinner.'

The response was either rude or irritated. Maheen rushed

to make amends. 'Do not get annoyed, please. I am sorry for asking. I only wished to serve your dinner.'

Her husband had hung up. Maheen put the phone down and hung her burqa in the cupboard. Her salwar-suit was drenched in sweat from all the shopping. Black clothes, like the darkness, absorbed whatever was poured in, not allowing anything to peep through. Neither wind nor light, neither thought nor vision, leaving one feeling caged but secure.

Maheen wiped her forehead with a towel and checked the front door. Good, it was locked. All the curtains were drawn. Finally, she switched on the television and put on DD Urdu.

Two women, dressed in almond-coloured salwar-suits, sat talking on a couch. Their heads were covered with hijabs. Maheen looked at them with respect. The 40-inch television was Maheen's best friend. It was wall-mounted and she had tastefully decorated the space. Right in front of the television was a brown sofa. On either side sat two flower vases with red and green plastic flowers. But she had other things on her mind. Maheen turned up the volume to the loudest setting, checked the door and the windows once again and disappeared into her bedroom.

On the bed lay the treasures from her shopping expedition, waiting to be tried out. The first bag contained twenty packs of fairness cream. She unscrewed one tube and put a little on her face. Then, she took off her white salwar-suit and put on her new bra. She admired herself in the mirror.

In the drawer of her bedside table was a measuring tape. She measured the width of her upper waist—it was thirty-six inches. How about her thighs? Twenty-four inches. *It should be the other way around*, she thought. Clenching her fists in dismay, she observed the wrinkles on her back. Her skin needed work. While the fairness creams had made her skin fair and smooth, the overall impression was that of a fair, sixteen-year-old head fixed atop a dark, forty-year-old torso. *Perhaps I should start applying the cream to my body*, she thought. Quickly, she emptied the tube by using the cream on every inch of her body.

'Much better,' she told her reflection. She was told by the society she was born into that fair is equal to beautiful. After all, whether it was the soul or the flesh, white was beautiful. It was only logical that white would be the colour of God, not the miserable black.

After completing her skin-care routine, Maheen decided to try on the frock. It was just like the one she had seen in a fashion magazine. While she did not consider herself a model, the dress suited her well. She was certain that her husband would start admiring her when he saw her in this frock; after all, she only bought it to grab his attention. She was busy admiring herself when the conversation between the two women on television caught her attention.

'O Prophet,' one of them was saying, 'say to your wives and your daughters and the women of the believers that they let down upon them their over-garments; this will be more proper, that they may be known, and thus they will not be given trouble; and Allah is Forgiving, Merciful. (Surah e Ahjab, Rukuh 8, Ayat 59, Quran Majeed.)'

The other woman added, 'Muslim women must protect themselves from this cosmetic world. Satan is all-powerful. He wishes to fill you with lust and pull you away from Allah!'

A shiver went up Maheen's spine. She could feel her delight slipping away. How sinfully she had been behaving! In a tizzy, she took off her frock and bra and put on the sweaty salwar-suit again. She picked up a pair of silver earrings and some bangles from her dresser. Then, she examined her hair and decided to wear it loose. Finally, she placed a hand on her chest and, after taking a deep breath, prayed to Allah for forgiveness. Her shopping bags, with all the fairness creams, powders and garments, were tucked away at the back of her cupboard, with her hopes.

The television was still blaring in the living room. One of the women, in an urgent tone, declared, 'We must be obedient wives because they feed us, clothe us, give us a roof over our heads and provide for our children.'

The other woman, nodding enthusiastically, quoted from the Quran, 'Your wives are as a tilth unto you; so approach your tilth when or how ye will; but do some good act for your souls beforehand; and fear Allah."

'Well quoted,' agreed her companion. 'Men are the protectors and maintainers of women because Allah has made one of them excel over the other. And because they spend out of their possessions. Thus, righteous women are obedient and guard the rights of men in their absence under Allah's protection. In the Quran—Surah Nisa, Rakuh 6, Ayat 34—it says, "As for women of whom you fear rebellion, convince them, and leave them apart in beds, and beat them. Then, if they obey you, do not seek a way against them."'

Maheen was so engrossed that she did not hear the persistent knocking. Gosh, it was two in the morning! She rushed to the door, hoping it was her husband and praying that he wouldn't be furious.

'I have been knocking for fifteen minutes! Where were you?' Jahangir Khan yelled as soon as she opened the door. The voices on the television reached his ears. 'Why does this idiot box run all the time in my house? All you women want to do is rest. You do a little dusting here, some cooking there and then watch television the whole day!'

Maheen stood with her head bowed, patiently waiting for him to finish his nightly rebuke. Every night she hoped that he would notice her silver earrings or compliment her on her fair skin. But that had not happened.

'Shall I serve dinner?' Maheen asked quietly after a while. She had grown to accept his grumpiness. After all, he worked hard all day.

'Have you eaten?' Jahangir enquired while changing into pyjamas. 'Or has the television filled up your belly?'

Maheen was elated to note the concern in her husband's voice. Her Jazzi was caring. She picked up his clothes, socks and undergarments from the floor. He was just short-tempered at times.

'No,' Maheen replied. 'I thought we could eat together.'

'How many times have I told you that I don't appreciate this show of love and affection? I usually eat at work. Haven't you understood this simple fact after one and a half years?'

She stayed silent. Jahangir lay down on the bed and Maheen rushed to cover him with a comforter. Perhaps now he would notice her make-up and jewellery. But Jahangir was glaring at her.

'Where were you this evening? Why were you roaming around outside all alone? This is Mumbai, not your dismal Habibganj.'

'I was not alone,' said Maheen, praying that this would not lead to an argument. 'I had gone out with the lady who lives in the flat opposite ours. Her name is Meera.'

'So?' Jahangir snapped. 'Who knows what kind of woman

she is? She isn't married but has a regular male visitor. Doesn't that tell you anything, you stupid woman?'

'He is her fiancé.'

'He is not her husband!' Jahangir shouted. 'How can Allah allow this kind of behaviour before marriage? Listen Maheen, you must not let the vices of this city lead you astray. You don't have much of a brain but you don't need much of it to wash dishes. All you must remember is not to sin. If you do,' he added threateningly, 'then you will face hellfire. I will ignore you completely while enjoying the fruits of heaven.' He turned away from her, drew the comforter up to his face and closed his eyes.

'You must be tired,' Maheen tried to placate him. 'Shall I massage your feet?'

'No,' he replied gruffly, keeping his eyes shut.

She continued talking, hoping to turn the conversation to a lighter subject. 'The milkman has upped his price again. I scolded him for cheating us. You work so hard to earn a living and he wants to steal our money!'

Jahangir didn't respond. 'Ammi called,' Maheen went on. 'She was saying we haven't visited her even once since the wedding.' Nothing. 'I had prepared *sevaiyan* today. I know it's your favourite dessert.' More silence. 'Do you remember you had gifted these earrings to me last year?' Jahangir was snoring.

Maheen gazed at Jahangir, and wiped away a few stubborn tears that had escaped her eyes. Taking off her jewellery and switching off the night light, she lay down on the bed. The black ceiling fan whirred overhead, the sound lulling her to sleep.

※

'*Jannat* reserves *hoors* for men and one sincere husband for each woman.' There was a new guest in the television studio that day. She spoke with an air of authority.

'With due obedience to Allah, why are there multiple virgins for the men but only one man for each woman?'

Maheen was listening intently. 'The physical needs of men are more intense,' explained the special guest. 'But Allah is generous and considerate toward everyone. For instance, he knows that women have a great fancy for jewellery. So, he gifts many ornaments to the women in Jannat.' The woman laughed as she said this. Maheen's face broke into a smile.

The clock had struck midnight, but Jahangir was nowhere in sight. Maheen was sitting on the couch, impatient. She had dressed up in a green salwar-suit and plastered her face with make-up. Growing bored of DD Urdu, she decided to indulge in a guilty pleasure. 'Please forgive me, Allah,' she prayed and switched to a Hindi movie channel.

On the screen, a very handsome Shah Rukh Khan was embracing Kajol in a beautiful mustard field. Gently, he brushed aside a lock of hair from her cheeks. Maheen's eyes glittered as Shah Rukh kissed Kajol on the forehead and then on her cheeks. Ah! It was the famous movie, *Dilwale Dulhania Le Jayenge*. Maheen clapped her hands and was making herself comfortable when someone knocked on the door. Alarmed, she hastily turned off the television and rushed to the door.

'Do you seek permission from a djinn before answering the door?' asked a rather wobbly Jahangir before stepping inside. 'Why does it take so long every night?'

'Pardon me, ji,' Maheen rushed to apologize, 'I will be quicker next time. Shall I serve dinner for you?' Maheen made sure to shake her wrists while talking; the bangles clinked against each other and made quite a noise. Jahangir, however, didn't pay any attention and began his bed-time routine.

Maheen began to pick up after him and hurried to straighten the bedsheet. 'You said you would come early today,' she spoke softly, so as not to rattle his nerves. 'I wanted to go to the bazaar to buy groceries.'

'Oh, so now you want me to tend to the house as well?' Jahangir snapped. 'Shall I start cooking too? And how come we run out of groceries every other day? How much do you eat? You are blowing up like a balloon!'

Maheen changed the subject. 'Let me massage your feet,' she said, beginning to knead his soles. 'You must be tired.'

'Just leave!' He yelled, shoving her roughly. 'Let me sleep in peace.'

※

At around three in the morning, Maheen woke up with a start. She had fallen asleep after gazing at the black ceiling fan for hours. Now, in the dead of night, she felt him drawing close to her. Was Jahangir asleep or awake? Maheen didn't care; she was overwhelmed that her husband was brushing against her, breathing on her neck, inching close enough to kiss her. He did love her, after all!

Maheen closed her eyes and pictured herself in the mustard fields she had seen on television a few hours ago. Just like Kajol, she too wished to melt into the embrace of her Shah Rukh Khan, her Jahangir. She waited with bated breath for him to kiss her forehead, stroke her cheeks. But that shattered when she suddenly felt Jahangir's hand roughly groping her breasts. His other hand slipped under her salwar with a manic urgency. She realized with a pang that this was no mustard field.

Jahangir soon started pushing himself against her. He got

on top, coming down on his wife without stopping to think if this was something that she wanted. Maheen's lips quivered as she struggled to bear both his weight and the pain she had started feeling between her legs.

'Please don't,' she attempted feebly. 'Don't be annoyed with me. I had changed the television channel only because they were showing a Shah Rukh Khan film. Otherwise, I strictly keep myself away from Satan.'

Sweat trickled down from Jahangir's head onto Maheen's cheeks. Her hands lay limp on either side of her torso, unable to draw the strength to shove her husband off. She felt caged on the bed. The distance between the love that she dreamed of and the reality that was her life was so vast it was almost laughable.

Maheen licked her lips; her throat was parched. She grabbed a corner of the bed to steady herself. 'It was a romantic song,' she tried again, 'Shah Rukh hugged Kajol tightly in beautiful mustard fields and kissed her...'

'Will you shut up?!' Jahangir howled, aroused and irritated at the same time. He put his palm over her mouth. He was thrusting against her wildly by now, making her cry out in pain. She bit her tongue, clenched her teeth and sighed in relief only when Jahangir climaxed and left her limp and alone. Within minutes, he had turned away from her and was fast asleep.

Maheen got off the bed and picked up her salwar from the floor. Jahangir had taken it off roughly and her impeccably ironed salwar was now creased. She walked to the bathroom and stood in front of the mirror. There were lipstick stains around her lips from when he shut her mouth with his hand. Maheen wiped off the stains and splashed some water on her face.

Outside her window, dawn was swiftly approaching. It was

four in the morning and the black ceiling fan in her bedroom whirred away untiringly. She lay down beside Jahangir and shut her eyes. Perhaps, if she could not see, she would feel peaceful enough to sleep.

Veer Tries to Woo Meera

The New Year was approaching sooner than I had expected. It was almost time for me to return to Rishikesh but Veer was unwilling to let me go. 'Who says we need to have an arranged marriage?' he said to me playfully one day. 'Stay with me for a few more days, at least until the New Year. Please?'

'I don't know what to say, Veer,' I replied, secretly pleased. 'I'll have to ask my parents.'

'I am sure they will agree.' He added proudly, 'The New Year celebrations in Mumbai are the best in India.'

Not long after that, I returned home one evening to a spellbinding sight. I had been out shopping for groceries and the bags fell from my hands when I entered my apartment. All over the living room were glittering fairy lights and brightly lit lamps. From the kitchen came a delicious aroma; I think it was my favourite *kadhi chawal* in the making. But what I loved best were my favourite curtains on the windows: a shade of beautiful grey that complemented the twilight sky outside.

Smiling in anticipation, I walked to the kitchen. Veer stood with an apron tied around him, busily making chapatis. He looked handsome and sincere, working hard to surprise me. It made my heart flutter with warmth. Veer grinned when he saw me and pulled me in for a hug. His flour-covered hands caught in my hair.

'I have lit fifty lamps for you,' he spoke right into my ear. 'It took me more than an hour. I have also made your favourite kadhi chawal. Now, don't I deserve a prize for all my labour?'

At that moment, I would have given him anything he asked for. But I pretended to be nonchalant and said, 'If you are in such a hurry to get your prize, don't cook kadhi chawal before our wedding night.'

Veer ignored my nonchalance, or perhaps he saw right through me. Inching closer, he planted a deep kiss on my lips. I froze. My cheeks turned red and my heart beat wildly. How could I stop his advances without offending him, especially after he had given me such a heartwarming surprise?

'I am starving,' I said, gently pushing him away.

Veer brushed off my little protest. This time, he kissed the nape of my neck and stroked my back. He clearly didn't get the hint. I don't know why he never understood my point of view. It was important for me to wait until marriage before being intimate, but to Veer, I was simply old-school. 'Shall we eat, please?' I began again.

Reluctantly, he consented and set the table for dinner. Minutes later, we were sitting across from each other, licking the plates clean. Veer was an amazing cook; I had to grant him that. 'I envy you,' I told him, taking another ladleful of kadhi.

'Learn to cook it yourself,' he winked in response. 'I, too, am like most husbands, so do not be deluded.' I was puzzled by his advice. As I started clearing away the plates, I smiled at my good fortune. Veer would not be a typical husband; he treated me with respect and was willing to go the extra mile to please me.

I was oblivious to the ugly truths that would rear their heads in only a few days. I would sink so far into the abyss that the sun would be no more than a distant memory.

※

It was midnight. The moon gleamed in the night sky and my balcony sparkled in its silvery light. I was sitting on a jute chair when Veer came and joined me, settling down on the mat. Suddenly, he lifted me by the waist and pulled me into his lap. The distance between us diminished again and panic started creeping up my back. I felt like a tortoise that had withdrawn into its shell.

Veer flinched at my hesitation. 'Why do you always react like this? Your eyes are eternally screaming for me to leave you alone. I am not going to leave you, do you understand? Every inch is mine!'

'Veer, please,' I protested, struggling to free myself, 'may I sit beside you?'

'Forget all this,' Veer shrugged, brushing his fingers against my cheeks and neck. 'Tell me, where would you like to go for our honeymoon?'

I did not reply. I settled down beside him and watched the stars. Veer held my hands in his and looked up at the sky too. For us, it was rare to sit silently, holding hands. I cherished these rare moments, but I wondered what was going on in his mind. 'What are you looking at, Veer?'

'Me?'

'Yes. You.'

'Well,' Veer replied with a chuckle, 'I am looking at the fortieth floor of that high-rise building. You see the one I mean?'

I looked in the direction he pointed and saw a skyscraper. It was lit up with hundreds of lights. 'What's special about that building?'

'The lights in that apartment have just been switched off. I guess it's time for action!' Veer winked at me mischievously.

I was appalled. Here I was, admiring the moonlight and cherishing a quiet moment, but Veer's attention was centred on the neighbours preparing to have sex. Why was sex always on his mind? I decided to confront him about it. 'Veer, can I ask you something?'

'Of course. I will answer all your questions, my queen,' he nodded lovingly.

'We are very different people,' I said, looking at him. It was high time we straightened things out. 'Our ideas don't match, especially about being intimate before getting married. You could have found a woman whose ideas matched yours. You could even have found a modern girl who was still a virgin in Mumbai. Why did you agree to marry me?'

'You think any virgins can remain in the same city as Veer?' he winked notoriously.

I could see that he wasn't taking me seriously. Moreover, I was feeling rather uncomfortable. Did he mean what he said? I needed an answer. 'Please, Veer,' I insisted. 'I must know why you said yes to marrying me.'

'Okay, okay,' he replied with some irritation. 'You think I consented to marry you because you are a virgin. I mean, never-been-fucked. Is that right?'

'Never-been-fucked?!' I lost my temper. 'How disgusting you are, Veer!'

'No more disgusting than your question was.'

Sighing in exasperation, I accepted that Veer wouldn't give

me any straight answers. I changed the subject. 'Ma keeps asking me when I plan to get back to Rishikesh. She needs my help to prepare for the wedding.'

'The wedding is on 5 March. There are more than three months. Tell your Ma you aren't going anywhere until after New Year.'

I loved the authority with which Veer made plans for me. I also loved that he wanted to ring in the New Year with me. Veer kept his arm around my waist as he announced his plans for the celebrations. My silly heart instantly reacted to his touch, sending shivers up my spine and unrest through my body.

This time, I leaned in closer to him and whispered in his ears. 'Veer, on the night of our wedding, rose petals will be spread over our bed. With dim lights in our room and the promise of a new life together, you, wearing your Banarasi kurta, will hold me tight. Your fingers will be entwined with mine as you come closer and—'

'And?' Veer couldn't stop himself from asking.

'And you will assure me of a lifetime of togetherness. "Meera," you will say, "I shall always be with you. You shall reside in my heart through the good times and the bad." You will kiss my forehead, my cheeks, my lips. And then—'

'Then?'

'Then, we will make love.' I added mischievously, 'All night if you so desire. But until that moment, we shall stay apart.'

Veer didn't resist as I slipped from his embrace with a smile, walked to my bedroom, lay on the bed and closed my eyes. I heard him shut the front door before leaving. All I wanted to do then was slip into dreams and reflect on the evening we had just spent together. That night, as I slept, I could picture only Veer. No one else managed to seep into my thoughts, not Kalika, Maheen or Joe. I was lying in my apartment in Mumbai, but my spirits were soaring toward the moon.

※

I awoke late the next morning. Damn it! I detested late mornings; they messed everything up. I rubbed my eyes and cursed my bedraggled hair. I heard a voice call out from a corner of the bedroom, 'Good morning!'

I screamed in shock. It was Veer. What on earth was he up to in my bedroom? I looked terrible just then. He had caught me at my sloppiest.

'What are you doing here?'

Veer didn't respond but gestured toward the bed. It was strewn with rose petals. He was dressed in a white *Banarasi kurta* and had lit aromatic candles in the bedroom. A sweet, heady scent entered my nostrils and wiped the last remnants of my drowsiness.

Then, he sat down beside me on the bed, took my hand in his and whispered, 'Meera, I shall always be with you. You shall reside in my heart through the good times and the bad.'

Everything I had said to Veer the night before came to me in a flash. Those were the exact words I had used. Was Veer going to follow it up with what I had promised? Embarrassed and nervous, I sprinted toward the bathroom.

'Meera!' complained Veer. 'This is not done. I did exactly as you asked. You cannot go back on your words now.' He was standing outside the bathroom door, howling like a stubborn child.

'You are insane!' I screamed back. 'I'll meet you in the evening. Just leave now!'

Thumping his feet in mock anger, Veer left the apartment. I laughed like a lunatic as I thought about Veer's antics. It wasn't desperate, I knew. I found it quite adorable. He had put up a show to ensure I had a big laugh for many months.

Perhaps, I was beginning to understand, Veer valued relations of the flesh as a route to the soul. It was his love language, just like mine was affection or conversation. He was brutally honest about it too. My parents had chosen a fantastic, if non-traditional, match for me. I loved the thrill it gave me.

Roar of the Dark

31 December 2011

It was only six in the morning, but I was already at the beach, watching waves crash against the seashore. It was going to be a hot day in Mumbai. Over the past few months, I had developed an intimate relationship with this beach; it held many of my memories.

It was a bright morning! There was a beautiful aroma drfting in through the open window. However, this day felt different. I had a sharp, unsettling feeling in my stomach, almost like something sinister was about to unfold. It was the day of the dark Lord Saturn, who brings misfortune and a reversal of fate. But why was I thinking all this? I took the small statue of Mahadev and held it close to my heart in order to ward off those negative thoughts. I knew he was always with me.

In a few hours, I would start preparing for the New Year's Eve celebrations. Veer had been going on about this night for weeks. Two days into the New Year, I would take a train back to Rishikesh to prepare for the upcoming wedding.

I was content in the little haven that Veer and I were building. *Why had my life collided with Joe, Maheen and Kalika?* I wondered. I had met these women only a few months ago. How was it that our lives had become so interconnected that I couldn't free myself no matter how much I struggled? When I decided to return to my apartment, I didn't know that I would never be the same.

※

It was a special day for me: I had finally worn the black dress Veer had gifted me so long ago and had pestered me to wear. It barely came down to my knees, and the straps were so thin they were almost non-existent. But I hadn't had the heart to refuse Veer that night. To feel more comfortable, I had accessorized the dress with a black velvet scarf over my shoulders. I had also picked out a matching clutch and high-heeled sandals. The clutch was so tiny it couldn't even hold my house-keys, but apparently, it was in vogue.

The entire city seemed to have come out on the streets that night. Never before had I seen such crazy traffic; how did anyone get anywhere? We had been struggling to reach the party venue—a five-star hotel in Juhu—for over an hour. It was important to arrive before midnight.

Back in Rishikesh, we celebrated the new year on the morning of 1 January. My Ma prepared a special menu for the day, including my favourite kadhi chawal. I would stand for hours in front of Lord Shiva, making resolutions for the year ahead. Everything was so different here. My mind wandered to Joe. 'Will Joe be at the party too?' I asked Veer.

'Yes, she is at the same hotel,' he replied, his brows furrowed in concentration as he tried to navigate through the traffic. 'But she will join us later, after attending to a guest.'

※

Joe was lying unclothed on the bed. The silk bedsheet felt soothing to her forehead, which was starting to ache a little. A mild golden light illuminated her body. Five-star hotels sure knew how to get their bedding right. Jahangir was lying beside her, stark naked.

'Happy New Year, my love,' Jahangir whispered, stroking her buttocks.

'There's a whole hour to go before the clock strikes midnight,' replied Joe, her breath reeking of alcohol.

Jahangir's phone, kept on the bedside table, started ringing again. It was the fifth time it had buzzed in the last hour. Vexed, he put it on silent.

※

Maheen looked at her phone in dismay. Jahangir was not taking her calls. For the first time since her wedding, she decided to do the unthinkable. Pulling out a diary from the cupboard, she found a phone number written right at the end, hidden behind the cover. She dialled it, ignored the shivering of her hands and waited for a response. 'Ji, salaam. This is Maheen. I need your help.'

Fifteen minutes later, Maheen was sitting in the rear seat of a taxi. She was startled when she looked out of the window. Had the whole of Mumbai decided to go out? Behind her burqa, her eyes sparkled with a mix of amazement and fear.

A young boy, who was seated beside the driver, turned back and smiled at her. Maheen smiled back. She had known him for a long time now; he was the boy who frequently came over to deliver things for Jahangir.

It had taken a terrible incident in the morning for Maheen to step out of the house alone. 'Happy New Year, ji,' she had greeted Jahangir happily when he was getting ready for work. Bowing her head, she had added, 'I know it's a day in advance, but I wanted to be the first one to wish you.'

Jahangir had been combing his hair in front of the mirror. He had turned toward her and had stayed quiet for a moment. Maheen had waited in anticipation, expecting a rare smile, perhaps a gesture of affection. Instead, her husband had growled, 'Is it Eid today? Is it the month of Ramzan? After every 364 days, we get 31 December. What's the grand deal about it? I suggest you start keeping the company of decent people. It wouldn't take much to divorce you.'

Maheen had stood like a stone. Jahangir had used the word *talaq* for the first time in their marriage. To her, it was like a death warrant. How stupid she had been to annoy her husband! Her father had explained to her long ago that women were indebted to their spouses. It was because of a woman's folly that man had to descend to the earth from the heavens. Jahangir had stomped out of the room but Maheen had stood rooted to the spot, cursing herself. She had to seek his forgiveness at any cost.

The taxi screeched to a halt, bringing Maheen back to the present. The boy climbed down and opened her door.

'Would you please wait here for me? I won't be long,' she requested the boy.

He looked hesitant but relented. 'Madam,' he pleaded, 'don't tell Jahangir sir that I brought you here. He will be annoyed with me and I can't afford that. You have always been nice to me, so I couldn't refuse.'

'Don't worry. I swear by Allah that I won't.'

At the door of the hotel, Maheen shivered. How many sins was she going to commit that day? Since she was a child, she had never talked to an unknown man, let alone travel with one. She was outside the house without her husband's permission. But whatever she had done had been driven by panic. She was afraid of losing her husband. For once, her terror of loss had outweighed her fear of Allah.

As Maheen walked toward the receptionist, she tried her best to compose herself. Fear had won over men for generations. Great men had ruled over the earth by unleashing this weapon, hadn't they? Fear is, after all, a shrewd buyer. It sells itself to buy the world. It wouldn't do for Maheen to succumb to fear just then.

She took the elevator to Jahangir's room and prepared herself for what he might say. Jahangir may not be very affectionate, but he was a virtuous husband. He hadn't kept three more wives, although he was permitted to. What could this be attributed to, if not love? Moreover, she had been foolish to wish him in the morning. New Year was indeed a frivolous affair.

Maheen had been standing outside the door for five minutes, unable to muster the courage to ring the bell. Then, she noticed that the door was ajar. Before she could stop herself, she pushed it open.

The first thing her eyes fell on was Joe's naked body wrapped around her Jahangir. The two seemed to be embracing. Neither had noticed Maheen standing frozen in the doorway, her back against the wall, her feet rooted to the floor.

Joe was the first to sense another presence in the room. She broke free from the embrace to see Maheen standing motionless, sobbing noiselessly. The woman stood like a lifeless statue, unable to retreat or advance. Her eyes were full of disbelief and disappointment. Joe did not know who she was. She had never met her but she soon realized that she was looking at Jahangir's wife.

Unaware of Maheen's presence, Jahangir continued to kiss Joe wildly. He sucked on her neck, bit her shoulders and fondled her breasts. Joe seemed to realize that something was not quite right about the situation, but she was too drunk to do anything about it. With her fading consciousness, Joe continued to stare into those spiritless black eyes that were peering at her from behind the hijab.

All these days, Maheen had set her heart on the dawn she believed lay right behind the darkness. It would envelop her one day with sunshine. But the sight in front of her eyes was a testament to a perennial night. The sun would never rise for her.

Eventually, the mighty darkness that was descending upon Maheen also found its way into Joe's intoxicated spirit. It was as if *prana* was evacuating her flesh. She found herself becoming immune to Jahangir's lust, unable to dispel the apparition at the door. Was it fear? No. This feeble, helpless woman could hardly hurt a fly. Was it guilt? Not really. She had always known that Jahangir was a married man. He was merely the ladder to her dreams; she was the object of his lust. This had always been their understanding. Many people were living out similar deals. She had no reason to feel apologetic. But if it wasn't fear and it wasn't guilt, what was this woman doing to make her feel so blue? Why did her heart seem to be tearing apart?

Hoping against hope, Maheen still stood lifelessly at the door, waiting for Jahangir to turn around and tell her, 'I love you. I am yours. What you are seeing is only a nightmare.' She would forget everything and disappear behind those closed doors to her quiet, withdrawn world in which she worshipped her protective husband. But as she watched, Jahangir continued to hold Joe's curvaceous body in passionate waves of love-making—she never knew that he was capable of it. The two women stared at each other wordlessly for what seemed like an eternity.

※

'Why is the stupid lift not working?' Kalika cursed as she collapsed on the stairs. Her feet were swollen because of her high-heeled slippers. A few stairs below, her phone lay ringing loudly. She struggled to pick it up and screamed into it, 'What is it? What do you care where I am? Like every drunkard, I am sitting on the stairs of my building, trying to find my flat.'

Drawing up all the strength she could, Kalika heaved herself up. With shaking hands, she managed to unlock the door and wobbled into her apartment. 'Couldn't you drop me to my flat?' she complained, almost falling down on the bed. 'All four of you morons thought nothing of probing inside my skirt all night at the New Year's Eve party, but not one of you had the decency to pay up!' Kalika's head was throbbing by now. 'And why did you rascals give me so much booze? I couldn't even see the stairs and the damned lift was not working! I'm hanging up, Sukkhi. I am furious with you!'

Kalika stripped down to her underwear and switched on the laptop. Her room resembled a war-zone. The bed hadn't been made in days; the almirah and the other furniture in the room were covered in a thick layer of dust. But Kalika was so engrossed in her laptop that she didn't even notice.

She picked up a black feathery mask lying on her bedside table and put it on. The mask completely covered her face; only her intoxicated eyes were visible. Kalika took off her underwear and, wearing just the mask, clicked a nude selfie. Up it went on a wildly popular porn site, along with her personal information.

Name: Kalika Sherawat

Wait, that wouldn't do. She deleted it and typed 'Kitty' instead.

Age: 17
Colour: Brown
Email ID: hot.kitty@sexmail.com
Password: Hunny Jasmine
Charges: 10,000 rupees per night
She clicked 'ENTER'.

⚘

Veer and I had finally reached the five-star hotel. But the challenges were far from over: we needed to find a parking space. When I looked out of the car window for a suitable spot, my eyes caught a magical sight. The sea. It was the same beach I had visited in the morning. As our car moved into a corner parking spot, I had the sudden urge to walk to the shore again and touch the waves.

'We are going to be late, you daydreamer!' Veer shouted so I could hear him above the din of traffic. We were in the parking area of a forty-storey luxury hotel and loud music seemed to filter in from all around us. The party was on the terrace. Veer had promised to meet his friends before midnight, but it was 11:45 p.m. already.

'Isn't forty storeys too much?' I complained. 'Couldn't your friends find any other place?'

'Don't worry, Meera. It will take you only forty seconds to reach the top.'

'Okay, let's rush then. It's almost midnight.'

To my surprise, Veer clutched my hand and rushed toward the beach instead of the elevator.

'Where are we going?' I asked him, surprised.

'There is something I want to tell you before the New Year dawns. And I want to do it at the place where we first opened our hearts to each other.'

We stood on the silent beach, our bare feet touching the sand, the waves only inches away. Moonlight gleamed around us, contrasting with the golden glow emanating from the hotel behind. Faint music managed to make its way to our ears. I wondered if I was standing at the very spot where Veer had first told me, 'I am lucky to have you in my life.' How far we had come in the past few months! How excited I was at the prospect of starting a new life together! Veer clasped my hands; his fingers were warm and comforting.

'What is it, Veer?' I asked him softly. 'It's only five minutes to midnight. Your friends are waiting for us.'

'I know that the difference in our worlds worries you, Meera,' Veer said, looking straight into my eyes. 'You feel that I agreed to marry you only because you hail from a small town. Can I be honest with you?'

'Yes.' My voice was hushed, and my heart beat rapidly with anticipation.

'You weren't wrong. That was the truth, but only in the beginning. Today, I am mad about you. I am enamoured by everything you do, even your multi-coloured, long skirts.

Tonight, you have put on this black dress, but it hardly matters. You are special to me, exactly as you are. I have come to realize that lust will fade away one day. What will remain is love. And it is love that I feel for you.'

That night, with the sea thundering around us and the moon bathing us in its light, Veer, for the very first time, said, 'I love you, Meera.'

As the words left his mouth, the noise around me dissolved into music. Were those the proverbial violins I heard playing in the distance? The anxiety that had clouded my heart in the morning faded away entirely.

Veer loved me. He loved me! Our marriage was not just an arranged marriage anymore. It was a companionship founded on love. All my dreams were coming true right before my eyes. I was glad that I had stayed back in Mumbai for the New Year. Veer had assured me that the glittering celebrations in Mumbai could overcome even the deepest darkness in the heart. I stood there silently, overwhelmed, quite unable to respond.

The ringing coming from Veer's phone broke our reverie. I think it was now past midnight as the night-sky had started lighting up with fireworks. I was about to tell Veer that we should head back to the hotel, when suddenly, a glass bottle flew through the air and landed near my toes. It was empty and reeked of liquor. I turned to see a group of men staring at us; there must have been nine or ten of them. From their rugged appearance and torn clothes, I gathered they belonged to a nearby slum.

In Rishikesh, people often talked about the contrasting worlds of Mumbai. Almost every five-star hotel in Mumbai had a slum in its vicinity. The bigger the hotel, the denser the slums. I tried to ignore the group of men and took a few deep breaths. They were making me feel somewhat unsettled. 'Let's go back, Veer,' I whispered, holding his hand tightly.

Before Veer could react, another glass bottle landed at my feet, narrowly missing my toes. One of the men shouted, 'Hey girl! Put your hands in mine too, won't you?'

Veer tightened his grip on my wrists and shouted back, 'If I call the police, they will beat you nice and proper and bring you to your bloody senses. Buzz off, you illiterate hooligans!'

Both of us rushed toward the hotel. The seashore was deserted, and I broke into a cold sweat. It was a failed mission.

'How dare you call us illiterate?' one of the men stopped us in our tracks and thundered. 'You are loafing around with this slut and trying to threaten us with the police? Bloody son of a bitch! Bloody motherfucker! I'll kill you!'

Everything happened in a blur.

I couldn't believe how rapidly things had spiralled out of control. The men shoved me aside and started beating Veer with the empty glass bottles. Veer tried desperately to put up a fight, but it was a losing battle. His forehead was bleeding. Frantically, I looked at the road leading up to the hotel and spotted a car. Perhaps someone could help us. Trying to be discreet enough not to be noticed by the crazed men, I ran toward the road.

'Where do you think you're going?' Two men grabbed me from behind, clasped my mouth to keep me from screaming and threw me on the wet sand. I lay still and out of breath, my throat choked in fear as the men continued to beat Veer mercilessly. No one heard us amid shouts of celebration.

Veer was losing an insane amount of blood, but the monsters continued to thrash him with the bottles. I couldn't watch anymore, but I knew he was no longer conscious.

Two men stood over me now, with others joining them. One of them bent down and started groping my chest. He pushed the straps of my dress aside, his lecherous eyes peeking inside. I struggled to free myself, but they were too strong and too many. I was overcome with fear. I looked helplessly at Veer; his eyes were only partially open, but I could see that he was straining to reach out for me. 'I am sorry, Veer,' I said under my breath, with tears streaming down my face. I could not do anything to help him.

'Why are you looking at him?' Someone slapped my left cheek. 'It's time you pay some attention to us!' All the men had now surrounded me, leaving Veer unconscious and bleeding profusely. One of them grabbed my hair and, without warning, roughly put his lips with mine. I felt as if sludge had been forced down my throat. Someone else had started rubbing my private parts, tearing away my clothes and underwear. My blood boiled, hot tears rolled down my cheeks as my breasts were fondled and then cruelly crushed. The more I cried, the more they laughed. My body didn't feel like mine anymore. Instead, it felt like a dumpster on which people spat, stomped their feet and walked away. It left a bad taste in my mouth.

My mind refused to comprehend that I was being raped.

It felt like an out-of-body experience, like I was staring at a corpse. I was looking at the body of a woman lying on the seashore whose clothes had been torn off and her hair was dishevelled, only to realized that it was me.

The shock had started to set in. While I knew that I was still alive, breathing became a difficult task and my soul longed to leave my body. What had happened to me was too deep and difficult to fathom.

I had lost track of time. My naked body continued to sink in the cold sand. By now, the pain in my wounds had begun to subside; I was becoming numb to the pain. My legs, still wide apart, felt lifeless. My eardrums failed to pick up any sound. Were they jammed?

I looked around for Veer. Where was he? Was he unconscious or…?

I felt a sharp stab of pain on the left side of my chest. I tried to see what was causing the pain but any movement was still painful. My mind refused to believe that humans could do this to each other. Petrified, I had watched those leeches crawl over me. Those men had tried to suck the life out of my body. I felt maggots burying into my flesh. These creatures were all over my body, peeling my skin and biting me. A bat-like monster had breathed right into my throat, poisoning me from within, dumping me into the abyss, crushing my bones into powder. As I struggled to break free of the bat, my tired eyes caught sight of a silver pendant around its neck, constantly thwacking against my forehead. There, carved neatly into the locket, was Lord Shiva.

No! This was impossible! How could Lord Shiva witness my misery without doing anything? How could he do nothing, and actually be one with the monster? *Why* did the locket have Shiva inscribed on it when it could have been any of the thousands of gods that exist in the seven worlds?

The sight of Lord Shiva on that locket, the one God I had prayed to since I was a little girl, aggrieved me even more in my state.

I hadn't ever missed my Monday fast for Shiva. Every so

often, I would collect conch shells from the quietly flowing river in Rishikesh and offer them to my protector. I believed that as long as Lord Shiva had my back, no poison could touch me. With him as my guardian angel, I never had to be afraid. After all, it was on the mountain of Kailash, at the centre of the dark cosmos, that he meditated. He wore dark ash, and it was darkness that soothed me to sleep each night. Then how could the darkness turn against me? How could the dark turn humans into bats, leeches and maggots? How could the dark suck away all the light from me?

My childhood belief that I had a special connection with Shiva had been proved no more than wishful thinking. That night he was watching me without a hint of guilt, not reaching out to pull me out of my agony. Why didn't he save me, his ardent devotee, from being torn to pieces? What kind of God doesn't care about the dignity of his people? My eyes started to blur, my pain intensified. I was still surrounded by the monsters; the leeches were still sucking my blood. I could only see that shining silver locket. As it bumped against my forehead, I knew.

All my life, I had been living a giant lie. But I knew now that the darkness was nobody's friend. It was an all-powerful force that housed evil, criminals and mosquitoes. It did not comfort but was a place of distrust and misguided optimism. It did not mean tranquillity; it denoted destruction, fear and death. The slightest wind could extinguish the light, but darkness was permanent... Yes, indeed, the dark is demonic and the demonic is real.

Lord Hanuman is said to have swallowed the sun. But maybe the dark is too much for him to swallow. The all-powerful light is a hoax. The dark alone is the lord of the earth. I had witnessed the ever-expanding, mighty darkness overpowering Lord Shiva himself.

I cannot deny that I had been too immersed in the gifts of life—my perishable hopes and the childish dreams for the world that I would build with Veer. I had been blind to the cold fingers of the eternal darkness that were slowly strangling me. It only became apparent in the semi-conscious haze that followed after the last of the men had finished with me.

I would try to sleep, I decided. It shouldn't be too difficult, since both my body and soul were begging for release. I wished for a blanket, but the only cover I was going to get was that of the night—the impenetrable darkness that precedes dawn—and I lay there, begging for sleep, praying for death.

※

The night of 31 December brought doom not only upon me but also upon Maheen, Kalika and Joe. All of us were shoved into the demonic darkness and cruelly uprooted from our worlds. Doomsday, while birthing new life, is said to leave souls bleeding. What is 'creation' for God is sometimes 'destruction' for mankind. Were we to step into a new world or were we doomed to be eliminated?

I was reminded again of the lines I had written in what seemed like another age…

When something happens in life
That shatters the castle of my dreams,
The skies fall upon me,
And so distant my dreams begin to seem…
The chiming of whistles,
The roar of a new beginning…

Piercing through the heat of the day,
The deep dark shining...
They call the dark by many names:
Ferocious, demonic, inhumane.
Yet they all allude to the same:
Dumping the garbage of their own soul in the name.
The night, the evil, the insane.
But we bury the peaceful dead in the lap of darkness.
We close our eyes to welcome sleep.
The womb is dark. Shiva is dark.
You may fear the dark,
But in the dark, I thrive.

Kalika Begins a New Chapter

January 2012

'What's up, Kalika? You look super sexy!' Sukkhi, sitting beside Kalika on the bed, winked as he caressed her thighs. Kalika was wearing a loose cotton T-shirt and short white knickers. She put her legs in Sukkhi's lap.

'You think so?' She said, handing him a yellow envelope. 'Tell me how you like these pictures.'

Inside the envelope were several photographs of Kalika dressed in lounge wear, deep neck gowns, hot pants and a red bikini. Sukkhi's eyes bulged. 'You look like a bombshell!' he exclaimed. 'What a figure! Do you want to be a model now?'

'I can become whatever I wish. Do you doubt me?'

'Not at all,' Sukkhi grinned, sucking her big toe. 'Why don't you let me take a few pictures of you in a bikini? I want to be as fortunate as that photographer of yours.'

'You are way more fortunate than him and you know it,' she said giggling. 'Is there any part of my body that you haven't already seen?'

'But tell me,' Sukkhi persisted, 'who clicked these pictures?'

'Jahangir,' Kalika replied, trying to sound casual. 'He's really famous. They call him Jazzi in the modelling world.'

'Jazzi? You mean Joe's boyfriend, Jahangir? How did you get him to agree?'

'Well, let's just say he couldn't resist Kitty's glamour.'

'Ah,' Sukkhi sighed. 'Now I get it. You slept with him.'

'So? What's the big deal? Joe does it all the time.' Kalika said nonchalantly. She sensed that Sukkhi was not entirely pleased. 'Anyway, he is no "boyfriend". They only sleep together.'

Just then, Kalika's phone started ringing. She stared at the screen and turned white as a sheet.

'What happened? Who's calling you after midnight?'

'Shh! It's my Maasi,' Kalika responded in a hushed voice before accepting the call. 'Hello, Maasi, how are you? Are you coming home?'

Sukkhi sat silently as Kalika continued the conversation. She didn't sound pleased.

'But why, Maasi? Does *Mausaji* not need your help now?' She looked anxiously at Sukkhi.

'Am I alone? Of course, I am alone. I was studying and lost track of time. If you had told me you were coming home, I would have made dinner for you.'

'So, you burn the midnight oil, eh?' Sukkhi chuckled. Kalika let out a frustrated noise.

'Get out of my flat, Sukkhi. Maasi is coming back and you have no idea how many things will have to change. All my freedom is going to go for a toss.'

'Anything I can do to help?'

'Don't call me! Text if you want to talk. And tell your friends, too.'

'Okay, okay,' Sukkhi said as she almost pushed him out.

'Don't forget to change that stinking bedsheet of yours. It's soaked with my semen and you have been sleeping on it for months.'

'Get out!' Kalika slammed the door and surveyed the house. Gosh, it was going to need a lot of work and she barely had any time.

Frantically, Kalika began picking up things, rearranging others; cleaning this, hiding that. She peeled the English movie posters from the wall and replaced them with pictures of Hindu deities. The empty liquor bottles and cigarette packets she dumped in garbage bags. The wallpaper on her laptop—of porn-star Hunny Jasmine—was hastily switched to one of Kalpana Chawla, the great Indian astronaut.

By the time Kalika finished, an hour had passed. Maasi would be arriving soon and she still had to fix herself. If she saw Kalika wearing a T-shirt and knickers, she would be killed for honour's sake and her parents would applaud her Maasi for doing it! Hurriedly, she put on a blue salwar-kameez and hid all her cocktail dresses and skirts in a box under her bed. Finally, she lit a single lamp in front of the temple and heaved a sigh of relief. She was ready to meet her aunt. She would never know that anything had changed, that the girl she had left behind had disappeared and it was Kitty who now lived here.

※

When I think about how much Kalika had changed in the past few months, I find myself becoming judgmental. Watching her like a voyeur, I would enumerate all the ways in which we differed. This made me feel a little superior. Witnessing the downfall of a person has the peculiar effect of making people feel good about themselves. Then they are free to say, *I am not like her.*

But who decides what 'downfall' looks like? Someone's sin could be someone else's virtue. Perhaps, it would have been easier if the universe had handed down watertight definitions of what was virtuous and what wasn't. But the universe is lazy. With changing times, the morals and ethics of our society changed and everything we had once believed in dissolved into nothingness.

Humans have always been mere slaves to their circumstances, dancing to the tunes of the ever-changing rules of society. What meaning did their faith hold—it seemed only as significant as a footnote in the annals of history.

For years, I had thought myself an invincible magician who would always live by her faith. I wasn't afraid, unlike the people around me, and believed that I could turn twilight into dawn. But that last night of December, my conviction could not save me. In what would I rest my faith now? I was a victim of the horrific reality of a world where the body is more valuable than the soul.

Veer was right. How would I morph my morals into ones that could adapt to my new reality? If I ever wanted to look myself in the mirror, I had to let go of my fantasies. I had to come to terms with my transformed world.

ಞ

Pappu walked in with two large suitcases. Kalika's Maasi followed. Kalika did not like him at all. Pappu was filthy and always had too much oil in his hair. But he had seen Kalika's antics in her Maasi's absence. If he wanted to, he could rat her out and that would be the end of Kalika's life in Mumbai.

Pappu seemed to sense Kalika's discomfort and drew some pleasure from it. Sitting on the sofa, he grinned, the kind that screamed, 'I can make you do anything I want!' He accepted the glass of water that she offered and frowned. 'Arey Kalika, what type of dress are you wearing today?'

Kalika heard the taunt in his question, but Maasi seemed to have missed it.

'What's wrong with her dress?' Maasi asked curiously. 'What a beautiful blue suit she is wearing! Stop mocking my lovely niece. Would you like something to eat?'

'No, aunty. I don't want to eat anything. Thank you,' Pappu was enjoying the attention.

'Such a helpful boy you are,' Maasi smiled. 'God bless you. My back started aching in the train and then the cab driver was speeding as if his wife was in labour!' Maasi turned to Kalika, as if remembering something. 'Why didn't you come to the station to help me?'

'You did not tell me...'

'Stop arguing!'

Pappu stood up and stretched his arms. 'Okay, aunty, I will take your leave now. I have so much to tell you,' he added, while gesturing to Kalika, 'but you seem tired. I will come by later.'

'Sure, *beta*,' Maasi replied, settling down more comfortably on the sofa. 'Thank you for everything.'

Pappu left the apartment, giving Kalika another menacing grin. Maasi turned to Kalika and ordered, 'Make some lemon-water for me. It is so hot, even in January.'

Kalika, who was still thinking about the peril of insulting Pappu, now had two sides to her existence; while one caged her, the other liberated her—at least, that was what she believed. She knew she would have to hide Kitty from her family until she was as popular as Hunny.

As Kalika busied herself in the kitchen, her aunt began inspecting the house. 'This was the first time I left the house for such a long time,' she said, while examining the neat living room and the burning lamp in the temple. Maasi's eyes were as sharp as those of a soldier posted on the border. 'Mumbai to Pune, Pune to Mumbai—it's all too much for me now. I was thinking of selling everything and moving to Pune for good. Your Mausaji is unlikely to get a transfer so close to his retirement.'

When Kalika brought the lemon-water, she patted her head lovingly. 'My child has become very mature. So lovely the house looks!'

Kalika smiled in relief. Her aunt sat on the bed and Kalika massaged her feet. 'How is the nimbu paani, Maasi?'

'Oh, it's fantastic! You have done a wonderful job.' She added in a reminiscing tone, 'You know, Kalika, my cooking was the talk of the whole district when I was young. Boys queued up to marry me. Your mother sent you here to pick up such virtues from me. I came back only because you are my responsibility. You must learn all the skills you need to become a good wife so that we can marry you off into a reputable family.'

This conversation was going down a dangerous route. Kalika hated such preaching; she did not want a life like her mother, living at the mercy of an angry father. 'Maasi,' Kalika interrupted, 'you must be tired from your journey. Why don't you get some rest?'

Her aunt, who was fatigued, soon fell asleep. Kalika rushed to her room and switched on her laptop. Her bedroom was sparkling after several days; a crisp, green bedsheet complemented the off-white curtains on the windows. She grabbed her mask from its hiding spot under the tape-recorder and quickly put it on. Maasi had started snoring. Assured that she wouldn't be disturbed, Kalika took off her salwar-kameez and struck a provocative pose in her red lace lingerie set. Soon, several chat invitations filled her laptop screen.

raju@sexmail.com: You sure look hot! How much will you charge to get fully naked, honey?

hot.kitty@sexmail.com: 100 dollars, my love.

raju@sexmail.com: You seem to be Indian. Am I right? Show me your face.

hot.kitty@sexmail.com: Why do you need to see my face? You are only concerned with what is below my face. Come on, transfer the money quickly and I will get naked for you.

raju@sexmail.com: Oh my, my! Look at the tantrums of a prostitute!

hot.kitty@sexmail.com: Excuse me?! You cheap, rowdy man! I am not a prostitute; I am a porn star. Do you understand?

raju@sexmail.com: Okay, okay, my star! Don't be angry and get naked.

Kalika, letting go of her anger, obliged. She sat on her bed completely naked. Her screen was jam-packed with chat windows. She seemed to be getting quite popular.

For several hours that night, Kitty, the porn star, challenged the ethos of her community. She believed that she had a higher moral standing than a prostitute. The fish had fallen into the sticky tank, unaware of its depth. In the next room, an oblivious Maasi, snored away peacefully.

Joe Burns for Redemption

'No, no! It's not me who's on sale; it's the necklace I'm wearing.' Joe read the script cheerily, looking at the camera with confidence. 'Join the bidding and this necklace could be all yours. What are you waiting for? All you have to do is pick up the phone, dial the number and enjoy the luxury of teleshopping while sitting at home.'

Vinay, the assistant director of the advertisement, was observing her closely. 'Did I say that right?' Joe enquired after the shot.

'Yes, madam, you did great! This advertisement is going to rock.'

'Is Jahangir photographing the shoot?' Joe whispered, looking around the set discreetly.

Vinay did not respond. He was fighting a battle of his own—one that had started on the night of 31 December, when he had led Maheen to Jahangir and Joe's hotel room. Neither of them had been aware of this and he dreaded what would happen if they found out.

Vinay had been working with Jahangir for several years. While his loyalties rested with Jahangir, he couldn't help feeling sorry for Maheen. She was a simple, warm lady to whom destiny had doled out a great deal of rubbish. Immersed in his thoughts, Vinay sat unresponsively, wishing Joe would leave. But she prodded him again.

'Vinay! I just asked you something! Is Jahangir photographing this advertisement?'

'Y-yes,' he eventually responded. 'Jazzi sir is doing this shoot. Okay, madam, I will see you for the next shot in five minutes.'

Joe sat back on the couch. She was wearing a simple white saree. She was nervous and confused about meeting Jahangir. In the distance, she saw him talking with two men. The men looked like they were with the teleshopping company. She looked away hastily, unwilling to meet his eyes. She had begun to find Jahangir threatening after the events of New Year's Eve night. Whenever she looked at him, Maheen's woeful face came into view. She could see her crying, her tears cutting Joe's skin like a hundred daggers. That night followed Joe wherever she went.

'Joe? I have been calling you for the last five minutes!' Jahangir shouted. He was visibly agitated. 'You're delaying the shoot. Don't forget that you are also a part of the product. The product will sell only if your curves do. So, focus on the job that you have been paid to do.'

Joe's face fell. Jahangir hadn't behaved so boorishly with her in the last five years. It was disrespectful to be put down like that in front of high profile clients and a dozen crew members. Trying her best to regain her composure she stood up, gulped down her embarrassment and walked to the green room. Everyone except Jahangir stared at her awkwardly.

As soon as she was alone, Joe took off her saree, threw it on the floor and looked at her naked body with loathing.

The diamond necklace glittered around her neck. Before she could take it off, someone walked up behind her and wrapped a hand around her neck. She was taken unawares and almost choked.

'Why haven't you been answering your phone for the past ten days?' Jahangir roared. 'So what if my wife saw us naked together? Why does it matter to a girl like you? I practically picked you up from the roadside and made you into who you are today. How dare you refuse me, you bloody whore?!'

Joe's face turned purple as she struggled to breathe. She could barely stand, let alone respond. Jahangir went on without the faintest shred of compassion, 'Wives are the honour of men and girls like you exist for our pleasure. You understand this, don't you? Shove this into your head: let me handle my wife and do not dare to refuse me!' He spat on the floor, shoved her and stomped out of the room.

Joe collapsed as soon as he left, breathing in great gulps of air. A sharp pain gnawed at her chest. She felt like she was suffocating even though she was free to breathe. With shaking legs, she walked to the door of the green room and bolted it. There were red marks on her throat where his fingers had been.

Joe tenderly examined her neck and went over every word that Jahangir had said. She had seen herself naked many times, but she had never felt as vulnerable as she had in that moment. While Jahangir was enamoured with her, Joe knew that their relationship was based on an exchange. At long last, she had to confront this brutal truth which she had deliberately hidden from her conscience. But her conscience had made its way out and it gave off a stench. She had become a dumpster for Jahangir's ego. She did not mean anything to him. She had prized ambition above doing the right thing.

As Joe wiped away her tears and got dressed, she felt like she was on a precipice: a part of her way dying and another being birthed. She was drifting away from Jahangir. What was left in her life? What did the next part of her life hold?

※

Her car was parked in the basement. She opened the door and sat in the driver's seat. All she wanted just then was to leave the studio. Unmentionable fears were clouding her senses and she needed some time alone.

'Don't leave yet,' said Jahangir as he suddenly appeared outside her door. Had he been standing there all this time? Joe tried to lock the door but he was too strong. He forced the door open and dragged her out. Pulling her toward him, he started kissing her, biting her lips. An animalistic rage came over him. Joe, feeling helpless, lashed out with both arms. She tried to shove him away. She tried to escape but she was pinned between the car and Jahangir.

Joe's struggles seemed to please Jahangir. He tore off her T-shirt in one swift motion, leaving her bra exposed. She stared at him helplessly. Zapped of all energy, she was unable to protest anymore.

'If I can make you, I can also destroy you,' Jahangir smirked. 'I have kept you close all this while so that you can sit on my lap, not dance on my head. You are nothing more than a piece of flesh. I can devour you whenever I want!'

Joe opened her mouth to retaliate, but Jahangir wasn't done. 'What are women made for anyway? Food and sex! You are worth nothing more than that. All your fucking utility lies only in the kitchen and the bedroom!' Unable to contain his rage, Jahangir slapped her on the right cheek. His fingers left marks on her pale skin. But she stood silent, humiliated and hurt.

'Why don't you say anything? Don't stand there like a plastic doll. Speak, bitch! Tell me why you've been avoiding me!' Jahangir hollered once again.

Joe knew that Jahangir was not interested in the truth. He only wanted her to surrender to his whims. But she felt incapable of lying anymore. Joe felt as if her soul had left her body. The first time it happened was on the night of 31 December, when Maheen's eyes saw right through her. And that day, with her conscience holding her accountable, she decided to be honest.

'After that night,' she began feebly, 'I could not forget your wife's face. I tried so hard. But she looked so helpless... I cannot forgive myself, Jahangir. My conscience is haunting me.'

'Your conscience?' chuckled Jahangir sarcastically. 'Why was it silent all these years but only choose to reveal itself on that one night? You're a bitch! Do prostitutes like you even have a conscience?'

'Yes,' replied Joe. Her voice echoed through the parking lot. 'Prostitutes like me also have a soul.'

'I don't believe it. A woman who has been seen naked by millions suddenly pretends to be a chaste goddess? Hogwash!'

'It isn't, Jahangir Khan,' Joe looked him in the eye and spoke with newfound confidence. 'I have woken up after what feels like a deep coma; clothed myself after a long, tiring parade through which I have walked naked. I have realized that I need to be able to face myself in the mirror.

It's not you I have to confront when I depart this mortal world but my own soul. I suggest you start getting used to this new version of Joe.'

Jahangir looked stumped. She took the opportunity to free herself before her courage dissipated and got into the car. He stared at her as she revved the engine and drove away.

※

Joe was probably over the speed limit, but she didn't care. She zipped through the busy Mumbai roads, oblivious to the traffic and the chaos that ensued in her wake. Joe did notice that the streets seemed crazier than usual. *Which was worse,* she wondered, *the madness inside her or outside on the road?* For the life of her, she could not decide.

She parked her car outside a five-star hotel in Bandra. A valet rushed to open the door. Not returning his eager smile, Joe rushed inside and ran straight to the ladies' room. There were four full-size mirrors. But, finally, she was alone. For the first time in her life, she embraced the solace that came with being alone.

Tears continued to flood Joe's eyes. Turning the faucet on, she splashed cool water on her face. She took off her torn T-shirt and found the change of clothes that she always kept in her purse. Finally, she wiped off her mascara and put on her dark-shaded glasses. She wanted to hide her tear-stained eyes from curious onlookers. The darkness cages us, veils us, but also protects us.

Joe walked to the reception, feeling more like her former self. 'Which way is room number 2101?'

'There is a lift right there, madam,' the receptionist pointed to her right. 'The room is on the twenty-first floor.'

She nodded her thanks and headed to the lift. Joe hoped she looked presentable for what awaited her.

※

'I'm glad Jahangir arranged our meeting. Or else, it would have been my loss,' said Joe as she smiled at Shivraj, the occupant of room 2101. He was a tall, heavily built man dressed in a velvet nightgown. He picked up his whisky glass and moved closer to her on the sofa.

'That's for sure,' Shivraj said immodestly. 'I can get you everything you want. Of course, it depends entirely on whether or not you can give me what I want.' He gave her a naughty grin and lightly lifted her T-shirt.

'What do you think?' said Joe, putting on a coquettish expression.

'Well, my company is launching a new range of skincare products. But I cannot decide whether or not you will be a suitable model for the range because of all these clothes that you are wearing.'

'No problem. Let me help you decide.'

Joe stood, gave him a seductive look and began to strip. As Shivraj sipped his whisky, Joe removed every piece of clothing she had on and stood naked in front of him.

'Is this better?' Joe asked, striking a pose.

'I still don't think you deserve my brand.'

'Let's see what we can do to change that,' she said. Joe settled down in his lap and gave him a long, deep kiss. Incredibly aroused by this, Shivraj threw his glass to the floor and pulled her closer. Soon, he was on top and Joe was being crushed under his weight.

'I will make you the queen of the modelling world!' he

breathed heavily, squeezing her bosom. 'For you, crores will be nothing more than peanuts!'

Joe, trapped under his body, moaned mechanically. She kept checking the wall clock. How much time would he take to climax? But Shivraj, unbothered, continued to heave against her as if he had all the time the world.

Just then, Shivraj's phone started ringing, startling both of them. Joe, already distracted, casually glanced at the screen. What she saw sparked a chain of events that neither had thought possible. The screen said: '*Biwi* calling'.

Joe lost it, her breathing became heavy. Hysterical and perspiring heavily, Joe shoved Shivraj aside and stood up with a start. She hastily grabbed her clothes and started dressing herself with trembling hands. After staring at Joe's incomprehensible behaviour, Shivraj charged at her like a manic bull. 'What are you doing, bitch?' he hollered. 'We are not done here!'

Joe did not respond. She was ready to leave the room, wondering why her conscience had come barging in again. Shivraj had managed to get up and wrap the bedsheet around his body. His phone continued to ring in the background, oblivious to the pandemonium it had caused. Irritated by the ringing, Shivraj smashed the screen, finally stopping the background noise. Joe did not even flinch. She threw open the door.

'Hey!' Shivraj screamed, 'Where are you going? What the fuck is this?'

Joe, blocking out his screaming, walked out the door and rushed toward the elevator. Shivraj, clutching the bedsheet, kept shouting, 'You bloody whore! Stop right now or I will finish you! I will destroy your future and bring you to your knees! You will come begging!' It took Joe monumental effort to get into the elevator and leave the hotel. By then, she was in tears, unable to control her emotions.

As Joe was getting into her car, her phone rang. With a sinking feeling in her chest she answered the call. 'Hello?'

'Madam,' said a mechanical voice. 'I am calling to inform you that you have been dropped from the advertisement campaign for 'Aesthetic Jewels' that you shot for yesterday. Jahangir sir wanted you out.' A few seconds later, another call shook her from her daze, 'Hi Joe, I have been told to inform you that you are not being considered for the advertising campaign for the skincare brand 'Soft and Smooth'.' Her phone slipped from her hand and fell to the ground. The world had come plummeting down. She watched the phone screen light up with call after call. She was sure that they were all calling her to tell her more of the same news.

Her gut hadn't been wrong. She had struggled so hard to establish herself in the modelling industry. What hadn't she done to become desirable and loved? But her conscience was out to ruin everything. When she closed her eyes to sleep, she saw Maheen chasing her in her nightmares. Joe cursed her conscience. That moment in the hotel room had been her undoing. What could she do to heal herself, to bring her life back on track?

She slammed the brakes and dialled a number on her phone. Yes, this phone conversation might be able to heal her wounds.

'Hello?' a soft voice greeted Joe. 'Who is this?'

Joe cleared her throat nervously and asked, 'Are you J-Jahangir's wife?'

'Yes ji, I am Maheen. Who are you?'

How could she answer that? Maheen's voice had made that night come alive again in her head. Joe had been sinfully naked in front of Maheen. She was responsible for robbing her of her dreams.

'I am Joe. Don't hang up on me, please. I want to apologize to you. Could you please try to forgive me?' Joe did not realize when she had started sobbing, but Maheen replied in a voice that was unwavering.

'So far, I have been unable to forgive myself. How, then, can I forgive you? It was my fault.'

The line went dead. Joe's heart sank. What did Maheen mean? Why was she blaming herself, and why did she have to seek forgiveness? Joe would rather have had Maheen abuse her. If she had humiliated her and called her names, Joe would have been able to shake off the horrible feeling in her heart. But Maheen inexplicably blamed herself, robbing Joe of the opportunity to make amends.

Why was she getting so worked up about it, anyway? Joe reprimanded herself for having become so idealistic overnight. Sexual exchanges were common all over the world. Why was there a big fuss about the body? Moreover, it wasn't as if she had sinned alone; wasn't Jahangir also at fault, if not more so? Who decided what was good and what was sinful? Surely, no definitions could remain constant in an ever-changing world.

Regardless of all this, one thing that stayed unchanging was pain. Joe could escape people's fragile beliefs. But how would she escape the guilt of causing pain to a helpless woman? This was a sin and would always remain one.

Joe frantically rolled up the windows of her car, trying to shut out the world and buried her face in her hands. She hoped her tears would wash away her guilt and spiralling thoughts. But hours later, there she was at the side of the street, unable to stop her tears. The futility of trying to rid herself of the guilt made her feel helpless.

Maheen Is Engulfed by the Dark

Maheen was too preoccupied for phone calls. She had brought out her old sewing machine that had once belonged to her grandmother and was now working away on it, deftly and swiftly. It was three in the morning, but Maheen had neither slept nor eaten in hours. In her hands was a black cotton cloth.

As she sewed, the events of the past few days raced through her mind. What had she told her husband that night in bed?

'Please don't be annoyed with me. I had changed the television channel only because they were showing a Shah Rukh Khan film. Otherwise, I strictly keep myself away from Satan. It was a romantic song. Shah Rukh hugged Kajol tightly in beautiful mustard fields, kissed her on the forehead, then her cheeks...'

There was a lump in her throat which she felt was choking her, like a python strangles its prey. The needle of the sewing machine seemed to prick her heart just like it pricked the cloth, inch by inch. During the course of their marriage, she had lived in the hope that Jahangir would someday hold her in his arms, kiss her forehead, hug her tight and play with her hair. Maybe, he would kiss her hands and compliment her cooking. She hoped that they would whisper in each other's ears, cuddling in bed as the darkness quietly slipped away.

But each night after sex, Maheen would gather her clothes and kiss her own hands for comfort. She had started to believe that her husband was incapable of love; he knew only animalistic desire. Or did she have it wrong? Was lovemaking like this for everyone? The fancy love scenes shown in films had intoxicated her and obscured reality.

But the night of 31 December had scarred Maheen. How lovingly, how passionately her husband had been kissing that girl! It was evident that he wasn't incapable of being gentle. She had convinced herself that it was she who didn't *deserve* any emotion other than mechanical lust. She lacked something, which was why her husband never treated her with affection.

The needle slipped from her hand and fell to the ground, bringing Maheen back to the present. The cloth had long been stitched; but her feet paddled away on the sewing machine. Maheen looked at the black cotton bag she had sewn together and felt an overwhelming desolation. Jahangir had dropped all pretences. He hadn't talked to her in weeks and had stopped eating at home entirely. He ignored Maheen the best he could; he had even stopped shouting at her. She was convinced he was thinking of divorce. He was probably enraged that she had followed him to the hotel that night.

Maheen placed the tubes of fairness creams and the television remote in the new bag. Then, she tied a knot and shoved the bag deep into the cupboard. With the leftover black cloth, she covered the television in the living room. There! She would only wear black and it would take over all the things she had once held dear. Satan could harm her no more for she had renounced the earthly light with all its seven colours.

The clock struck four. Sleep had evaded her all night, and

now, with dawn approaching, she felt more awake than ever. She sat by the window, sipping tea and peering through the green curtains of the room. Perhaps the sun would rise early that morning.

'I have been utterly foolish,' she said to herself in an attempt to alleviate her loneliness.

'My husband provides me with food, a roof over my head and honour in society. I was born in Habibganj, but he chose me even though he could have found any girl in Mumbai. Ammi told me that a woman could win over her husband only by being obedient and servile. Men own us. After all, they provide for us. The holy book clearly says this. I shouldn't have gone to that hotel without his permission. How insulted he must have felt! This television made it easy for the devil to possess my mind. Watching Shah Rukh Khan's movies made me mix drama with real life. I am glad that it is covered now.' Spoken out loud, her thoughts began making even more sense to her. Indeed she had rightly caged the devil with a black cloth.

Maheen stopped talking when she felt a burning sensation in her chest. Damn it! The tea was too hot. She should have sipped more carefully. It was always her fault.

※

Maheen hadn't caught a wink of sleep in almost forty-eight hours. She was sitting quietly on the sofa, staring at the hidden television. Her eyes felt droopy. Sleep had finally decided to reward her with some rest. But the doorbell rang and her eyes popped open again. Who else could it be but Jahangir? Overjoyed, Maheen rushed to the dressing table to apply her fairness cream out of habit. But then she remembered that all her make-up had been stowed away in black bags. She rushed to the door, unwilling to make Jahangir wait.

'I have cooked your favourite meal,' she whispered nervously as soon as he entered. 'Won't you have dinner?'

Jahangir sat down on the sofa and glanced at the covered television. He looked calm. Feeling more confident, Maheen decided to use the opportunity to apologize. 'Please pardon me,' she said with her head bowed. 'I should not have come to the hotel that night. You have been looking after me so well, but I still sinned. I swear to Allah, I will never repeat such a mistake. Speak to me, please?'

Jahangir sat motionless for a while. Finally, he looked at her and said, 'Go and get ready. I will take you out for dinner today.'

Maheen could not believe her ears. She had not expected to receive such a gift for her apology. Not only had Jahangir pardoned her, but he was also treating her to dinner—she could not remember the last time they had gone out together. She rushed to the bedroom and started to get ready for the occasion. She would wear her green salwar-suit with the golden border and pair it with gold earrings. It was the first gift Jahangir had given her after the wedding.

It was late at the night, but the roads were packed with vehicles. Maheen sat patiently in the car, her eyes glued to the world outside. She could feel the cool breeze through the half-open windows. The winds delighted her, soothing her wounds and filling her spirit with an uncharacteristic buoyancy. Jahangir was listening to an English song on the car stereo. She could not understand the lyrics. But it did not make a difference to Maheen as violins played in her heart.

MAHEEN IS ENGULFED BY THE DARK

The car came to a halt outside a large hotel. Maheen saw that it was the same hotel where she had seen Jahangir with Joe on New Year's Eve. Dread filled her heart. Painful visions from the night kept resurfacing in her mind, but she tried to ignore them as Jahangir led her inside. She had to learn to follow her husband unquestioningly. He was an excellent husband who fulfilled all her needs. It wouldn't do to question his intentions and make irreverent demands.

Maheen kept quiet as Jahangir led her inside the same room where he had made passionate love to Joe. Her heart had been ripped to pieces in this very spot.

※

'Bring one plate of *gosht* kebabs, *murgh* masala, four rotis, rice, buttermilk and salad,' Jahangir said, handing the waiter a five-hundred-rupee note. He added, 'I expect fast service.'

'Sure, sir. And what would you like, madam?' The waiter turned to Maheen. She was sitting next to Jahangir on the couch near the bed.

'She will have the same,' Jahangir interrupted and waved him off.

Maheen was extremely nervous. She had tried to calm down, but the question kept returning: why had Jahangir driven for a whole hour only to bring her to this room? They had driven past several restaurants and hotels; why couldn't he have picked one of them? She glanced at Jahangir, who was quietly watching television. He had flipped through channels, but not paused at the DD Urdu channel even once.

The food arrived and Jahangir ate hungrily, not taking his eyes off the screen. A hush presided over the room, broken only by the voices on the television.

'Eat your food,' he ordered Maheen, noticing that she hadn't touched it yet. As Maheen obeyed, with quivering fingers, she accidentally spilt some buttermilk on the carpet.

'You'll take a lifetime to learn the behaviour of literate people, I am sure,' he mocked.

Jahangir sounded so bitter that Maheen immediately started dabbing at the carpet with her dupatta.

'Shall I bring you a broom so that you can clean the entire hotel?' Jahangir scowled. 'Useless woman! Sit back and eat your food.'

Maheen, once again, obeyed, resigning herself to a corner of the bed. It seemed unlikely that Jahangir would have a normal conversation with her that night.

***

A fashion show was on in full swing on the television, with the female models parading around in high heels and skimpy lingerie. Jahangir was sitting comfortably on the couch, watching television and nibbling on peanuts. As he gulped down his umpteenth glass of liquor, Maheen anticipated something untoward.

Suddenly, Jahangir looked at her and brought out his camera. 'Come here, my beloved wife,' he gestured.

Maheen felt afraid. Jahangir's voice was low, his tone mild. He was not behaving like his usual self. Maheen was terrified of him. Nervously, she got up and stood a few feet away from Jahangir.

'Not so far!' he tugged on her arm and brought her closer. Then, he looked in his bag again and, with a flourish, brought out the frock and lingerie that Maheen had purchased from the shopping mall in Bandra several weeks ago. She froze, unable to speak or breathe. She had no clue how he had found them. Was he offended? Was this some version of Judgement Day when she would have to account for her sins? If it were, she would never be able to attain *Jannat*. There was only one thing to do.

'Please pardon me!' Maheen wailed, falling at her husband's feet. 'I am a foolish woman. Please don't be angry with me...'

Jahangir replied stoically, 'Why are you asking for forgiveness? You seek pardon for one thing or the other every waking second.' His voice grew sharp and his eyes blazed with fury. 'Is a CD stuck in your throat? Does it keep playing each time you cross me?'

Maheen, incapable of framing a suitable response, looked at him meekly. Her silence provoked Jahangir further. He tore at the frock and ripped it to pieces. The lingerie fell on her face, still in one piece.

'Go on!' he shouted. 'Wear your favourite clothes and show me. Let me admire your fashion choices.'

For a moment, Maheen thought she had misheard. 'Ji?' she protested quietly, her face red with shame. 'How can I wear these...'

'Why can't you? If you could dare to buy them, surely you can wear them too.' Jahangir thrust the underwear into her hands. 'Now go and get dressed this. I mustn't see anything on you but this.'

Maheen felt as if she had arrived in hell. Why was Jahangir making her do this? She rarely dared to see herself naked, even in the darkness. How could she face her husband in a brightly lit room wearing only this flimsy underwear? Even during sex, she had never been completely naked; Jahangir could get what he wanted by undoing her salwar.

'Please listen to me,' she tried again. Her throat was parched, and only a croak came out.

'Shut up and do as I say!' Jahangir's voice was loud and demanding. She hadn't the courage to disobey him, nor could she bring herself to obey his command. Feeling utterly dismayed, Maheen started crying profusely.

'Please pardon me! Please! I will never go to the market without you. I committed a great sin by purchasing such dirty clothes. But trust me, I have never worn them. I went astray only because I thought you might love me more if I wore such clothes and...' Maheen was sobbing, speaking in short, breathless bursts with her head on Jahangir's feet. 'I know this was all the result of television. Satan tricked me into this! But from now on, I shall never wander from the right path. Please forgive me...'

'This melodrama will not change a thing. But you are right. I will love you more if you wear clothes like these.' Jahangir was unfazed and pushed her aside roughly. 'Now get out and do as I say. If you argue any more, be ready for the worst.'

Maheen wiped her eyes and, with trembling feet, walked to the bathroom. Her husband had refused to hear her pleas, and she was compelled to do as he said. After all, she had committed an enormous sin.

Fifteen minutes later, she emerged from the bathroom with a towel wrapped around her body. Jahangir, who had been adjusting the lens of his camera, scowled at her. 'Drop the towel.' His thundering voice gave her no choice. She stood there in the maroon underwear, feeling exposed and humiliated. Her abdomen felt flabbier than ever and she had never detested her ill-proportioned curves more. Once again, she burst into tears of shame.

'I am feeling very ashamed, ji,' she wailed. 'Please allow me to wear my clothes. You are my husband; if you don't understand me, who will? I beg of you!'

'Shut up, you ugly, illiterate woman! I have had enough of you.' Jahangir brought out a package from his bag and handed it to Maheen. 'Look here, my dear wife,' he said sarcastically, 'I got you a pair of high-heeled sandals. Wear them and do a catwalk for me, just like you saw the models do on the television earlier. Let me enjoy the glamour of your advanced choices.'

Maheen ducked to avoid being hit by the shoes that Jahangir flung at her direction. She stood as speechless as a mannequin, feeling stripped of all her dignity. Although she was in a closed room, she felt as if hundreds of eyes were leering at her, commenting on her curves, making obscene remarks. 'I am sorry...' she started helplessly once more, but Jahangir shushed her rudely.

'Turn your tape recorder off! If you repeat your apology one more time, I won't leave even these clothes on your body. Now, put on the sandals and start walking.'

Her eyes were flooding with tears. Maheen bent and tried to put on the strappy sandals Jahangir had thrown at her. She had never put on such footwear before. How did anyone walk in these? With great difficulty, she stood and took a step. Immediately, she tumbled forward. Jahangir smirked and was about to make a snide comment, but Maheen adjusted her posture and resumed her walk.

'Very good!' said Jahangir as he clicked her pictures. 'That's my model wife!' His camera captured Maheen from all angles, recording her tears, humiliation and pain.

Maheen could not look at him. She tried to cover her bosom with her hands, making a vain attempt at restoring her sense of dignity.

'What are you doing?' He immediately shouted. 'You have such an awesome figure. Keep your hands away from your body!'

She knew her husband was taunting her as he shredded any respect she had for herself. She did as he asked, posing in her underwear and sandals, oblivious and numb to everything. Her feelings did not matter; the tears had stopped falling.

Jahangir cupped a layer of flab on Maheen's belly and commented sarcastically, 'I didn't know that my wife looked super-hot without clothes. I had uselessly been running after those models. It was my mistake. Your poor husband should have just looked under your salwar.'

This was the last nail in the coffin. Maheen had thought that nothing could affect her anymore, but Jahangir's final taunt shattered her entirely. What did a woman have if she couldn't respect herself?

'I can't bear this anymore,' she howled, hiding her face and falling to the floor. 'I feel as if I am being raped. I know I don't deserve you. I am not worthy of being loved. Anything you want, I accept. Please forgive me now.'

Jahangir looked at her with disinterest. He lifted her, seated her on the couch and covered her haphazardly with a bedsheet.

'What didn't I do for you?' He said, his voice low but stern. 'I picked you up from a garbage dump and gave you a fantastic home. How much did you study? Zero! How about your looks? Poor! Allah must have had a good reason to give you the complete package: low status, poor intelligence and below-average features.'

Maheen stared at the floor, crestfallen. Under the bedsheet, she brought her hands together and clasped them tightly.

'You keep applying fairness creams all the time. Have you tried them on buffaloes? Did they turn white? Who do you want to impress with your gaudy make-up? If I had been allergic to your appearance, I wouldn't have married you in the first place!'

'You are right,' she nodded. Everything Jahangir said made perfect sense.

'I married you because you were a God-fearing, obedient woman. I thought you would serve me well, and I would look after you and give you food, clothes and shelter. I am fulfilling my responsibility, but what are you doing? Hanging out with unworthy people! Spying on me! You know I am allowed to keep four women.'

Jahangir was ruffling deep-seated fears in her heart. She used to brush them off; preferring to live in a constructed reality. If she hadn't believed that Jahangir loved her, how would she have survived this long? But the truth was out—straight from the horse's mouth. Her husband felt no love for her. All her efforts had been in vain. Maheen raised her eyes; her tears had run out. The white sheet offered some modicum of protection. She managed to find some relief in the naked truth staring her in the face.

Jahangir was in no mood to soothe her hurt. 'Tell me,' he ordered, 'what does your husband do for a living?'

'You take photos,' she whispered.

'Okay. What do you call a man who takes photos?'

Maheen tried to remember the English word for his profession. 'Pho…photu…grapher, ji.'

'He's called a photographer! You can't speak even a single word of English. But that didn't stop you from spying on me.'

'I wasn't spying,' said Maheen. She was dismayed that he

had misinterpreted reality. 'I had come to apologize to you for my behaviour that morning.'

'Shut up!' Jahangir tore away the bedsheet and grabbed the lace underwear Maheen was wearing. 'Is this what your mother taught you? You fall prey to the devil's designs and succumb to the glittering attractions of this world. Why then should you expect to be rewarded with a noble husband like me? I am warning you for the last time, Maheen. Remain true to yourself. If you demand more than what you are getting, I will happily divorce you. Then you can dance to all those vulgar songs of Shah Rukh and Kajol freely.'

Maheen had started sobbing again, drenched in guilt. Would her tears never stop? 'I got misled,' she howled. 'I will never repeat this.'

This time, he relented. Jahangir made a great show of forgiving her for her monumental sins. Slowly, he inhaled a large gulp of air and let it out, pretending to release his wrath. Then, he nodded ever so slightly and gestured to Maheen to leave the room. She was glad to obey. With shivering hands she wrapped the white bedsheet around herself like a burqa. White was her favorite colour. She didn't know that it would help to save her from eternal shame.

As Jahangir settled down to watch television, Maheen, sobbing again, walked to the bathroom and shut the door. On the TV, a monkey was dancing to the tunes of a tall man brandishing a whip. Jahangir chuckled at the sight; his face glowed with narcissistic warmth and his eyes sparkled with pride.

※

In the early hours of the morning, Jahangir lay on the bed, snoring contentedly. Maheen lay next to him, unable to sleep.

Not being able to get any rest had become a routine part of her day. Back home, she would stare at the ceiling fan until her eyes drooped; here, she could only stare at the false ceiling. Although the room was air-conditioned, she was drenched in sweat. The fan in her bedroom at home was far superior to this fancy air-conditioning.

Maheen gave up; sleep seemed impossible just then. She got up from the bed, tied the knot of her salwar and walked to the posh bathroom.

Like the air-conditioning, the bathroom also seemed fancy but useless. Why would anyone build a glass washroom with full-length mirrors? Who wanted to stare at their naked bodies while showering? Thankfully, she was fully dressed now in the green salwar-suit she had carefully picked for the night.

How had things gone so wrong? It was only a few hours ago that she had been brimming with excitement. She had dressed in the clothes and accessories that Jahangir had gifted her after their wedding. She thought that they would have a candle-lit dinner. Jahangir would treat her with love and affection and all the misunderstandings of the past few days would dissipate! How foolish she had been... She stood alone, watching the gleaming marble bathtub. Joe might have bathed in it on New Year's Eve. Had Jahangir also entered the tub? Had he soaped her back and caressed her wet hair?

Everything had gone awry because of that cursed lingerie and frock. She had pictured her husband opening his heart to her when she wore it. He would find her as attractive as the beautiful women with whom he worked in Mumbai. But she should have known that nothing could change what was written in her destiny.

Maheen grabbed a pair of scissors from the bathroom

cabinet. In a fit of desperation, she cut the underwear into tiny pieces. Her efficient hands that moved so swiftly on a sewing machine trembled while holding the scissor. Ever since her honeymoon, she had dreamt of a night when she would undress completely and surrender herself to her husband. That night, her dream had come true. But it had been a nightmare in which she was unclothed by a stranger in front of gaping, obnoxious people.

Maheen dropped the shreds into the toilet and flushed them. She returned to the bedroom eventually and fell into a fitful slumber. Her dreams had evaporated; she didn't think she would ever find the courage to dream again.

All through childhood, she had heard stories of how happy, peaceful and abundant heaven is. If she wanted to reach heaven, she had to find a way to keep her faith. These stories helped to keep her going. She was sure that the other world would bestow upon her what she lacked in this one.

Stories bring hope. Hope is far superior to truth because it brings solace.

A New Reality for Meera

February 2012

Many sunrises slipped by unnoticed; many nights disappeared without sleep. In my apartment, a thick layer of dust had settled over the idol of Lord Shiva. I hadn't lit the lamp in several days. As another morning dawned and sunlight flooded the living room, I stirred a little. I was lying on the bed, hidden under my floral cotton comforter. To a spectator, I could be asleep or unconscious. I hadn't slept at all the night before. The sunshine did nothing to lift my spirits.

Lately, I had taken to sleeping during the day and staying up at night. I would watch television, flip through the pages of old books or sip water to soothe my eternally parched throat. Some nights, I would toss and turn in bed, occasionally laughing hysterically. If you were to ask me why I laughed, I wouldn't have an answer.

The slightest sound made me panic. A footstep or even a shadow could set off a full-blown anxiety attack. In the quiet of the night, my mind would involuntarily recreate the noise of crackers, the beeping of unfriendly horns, the crashing of waves against my naked body. Sometimes, I could swear I felt that dreadful silver pendant striking my forehead; Mahadev staring at me unblinkingly.

I had felt dead inside for so long that I had nearly forgotten how to live. A new year had begun, but it felt like an invasion. I questioned my whole existence; how could I climb out of an abyss that only wanted to pull me into its depths?

I forced myself to get off the bed and walked to the bathroom. Fearfully, I glanced at the mirror. My wounds stared back at me. The gash above my right eyebrow had healed; the teeth marks over my neck bones had also faded away.

I decided to bathe—the first in several days. Turning on the geyser, I stood under the shower. Water washed over my head, soaking my forehead, eyes, cheeks… Some of it pooled near my feet. It had been days since I had soaped my body; nothing seemed to matter anymore. I shut my eyes and allowed the water to cleanse my soul. All I wanted was for the water wash away my pain and the memories that haunted me every minute.

Suddenly, I felt a sharp, burning sensation. I realized that I turned the hot water tap on but not the cold water tap. I tried to turn on the cold water. The water was scalding my skin. My legs felt glued to the floor and I was not able to move away from water stream. Frantically, I tried to turn the shower off. I saw my naked reflection in the foggy mirror. There stood a shadow of the person I had been, reduced to a feeble, constantly afraid woman.

I was immediately taken back to that night on the seashore. It returned all at once: the crackers, the silvery moon, the monsters who tore at my clothes while wearing a pendant with the face of Mahadev engraved on it… My hands and feet froze.

I was unable to escape the boiling water. The bathroom was filling with steam and my skin was turning red. I screamed in pain when I could not take it any longer. I turned off the shower and rushed out of the bathroom. I caught sight of myself in the bedroom mirror: I was a spectre of myself, a hollowed-out version of the person I used to be. Was I going insane?

I grabbed the bedsheet from the bed and threw it on the mirror. It wasn't a permanent fix, but I couldn't stand the sight of my decomposed self for another moment.

※

My phone was ringing. I ignored it, focusing instead on the cup of tea in my hands. The warmth emanating from the teacup soothed my nerves. It was past three in the afternoon, but I felt no hunger, even though I had skipped breakfast. This wasn't new; lately, I felt hungry only in the evenings and ended up gorging on junk-food.

The phone started ringing again. I turned on the television to distract myself. Out of nowhere, thoughts of Joe entered my head as I switched aimlessly through the channels. I hadn't seen her in weeks. What had happened to Kalika who lived in the flat opposite Joe's? And what about my neighbour who had taken me shopping? I hadn't seen Maheen in many weeks.

I used to frown at the thought of having to stay in a closed apartment and not venture out. But my life had somersaulted in such a way that the courage to walk outdoors had left my body.

A breaking news report on television caught my attention.

'In a village in Uttar Pradesh, four men raped a six-year-old girl in broad daylight. The rapists are absconding. The police

are working round-the-clock to trace the culprits.'

I listened with growing horror as the anchor continued, *'The victim's four-year-old brother witnessed the incident. He covered his unconscious sister with a sheet and brought her home in a bullock cart. The girl has sustained multiple injuries on her body.'*

I shivered and turned the off the television with trembling hands. I could not see anything through my tears. How had Veer managed to lift me and seat me in his car? He had been severely injured and must have lost a lot of blood. Veer must have covered me with my torn clothes. Blood must have been oozing out of our wounds. How had he kept up his nerve while also shielding me from onlookers? I had remained unconscious for four days, Veer had told me. Through countless doctor visits and sleepless nights, he had tended to me, crying silent tears after seeing my lifeless, injured and violated body on the bed. A month had passed since the incident, but sand continued to show up in various corners of the house. It reminded me, as if I needed reminding, that the scars from that night would never leave me alone.

My breathing turned frantic; my veins throbbed against my temples. I was cursing myself for switching on the television when someone rang the doorbell. I wasn't expecting Veer, so who could it be? Fearfully, I peeped through the keyhole, but could not see anyone. Perhaps I had imagined it. My eyes fell on the lemon-and-chilli string I had tied to the doorway. It had dried almost completely, much like my reserves of strength. I took a deep breath to steady myself. I decided that I would go out and buy some groceries to avoid my nocturnal binge-eating.

❧

I entered the crowded lift. There were least five men in the elevator. I worked hard to suppress the panic that was building inside me. After all, I knew all these men. They were residents of my building and I had even talked to some of them before. They weren't out to harm me. I felt almost disgusted with myself for being so timid. It wasn't like me at all.

'How are you doing, beta? I haven't seen you in a while,' asked an elderly man just before the lift reached the eighth floor. 'Where is Veer?'

It was a simple, genuine question. But I could not bring myself to respond. Instead, I found myself doing something completely absurd: I pressed the stop button. I pushed through everyone standing in front of me and rushed out. As the occupants of the elevator stared at me quizzically, I wanted to scream and say, 'No, uncle! I am not well!' I wished I could tell the kind man who had asked after my well-being that I couldn't sleep at night anymore and that I didn't feel alive. Every waking minute, I felt suffocated. I feared the dark that I once cherished. Evenings depressed me; I was terrified of any man I met.

I also wanted to tell him to take me back to my world, my Rishikesh. 'Please take me back,' I wanted to tell him, 'I wish to die.'

But I said nothing. I stayed rooted to the spot as the doors of the elevator shut, and it continued its descent.

❧

I detested the traffic in Mumbai. In the past hour, a score of vehicles must have passed my autorickshaw. Everyone appeared to be racing to reach their destination. The sight of all those people in their big cars filled me with dread. What if someone pounced on me through their window? The auto-driver was also a suspicious man; every so often, he would glance in the rear-view mirror. Why did he need to look back so often? After all, we were moving forward!

'Madam ji!' The auto driver almost shouted. I had a feeling that he had been trying to get my attention for a while. 'You have been taking me round and round on the same road for an hour. Where do you want to go?'

His question took me by surprise. I thought I had made myself clear. Had we been wandering along the same road for an hour?

'*Arey* madam, why don't you speak? Where do you have to go?'

'I already told you I have to go to Bandra.'

'When did you say that?' The man sounded miffed. 'I have asked you at least ten times! Anyway, where in Bandra should I take you?'

'Bandra West.'

'What?!' He was utterly irritated. 'You got in over there,' he pronounced each word slowly. 'Do you want me to take you back?'

'Yes.'

'What is this, madam? Why did you get in if you did not have to go anywhere?' He added under his breath, 'What insane people I come across in Mumbai...'

I finally lost my temper. 'Are you taking me for a free ride?' I thundered. 'And why are you looking at me repeatedly from your rear-view mirror? Do you think I am too naïve to understand your intentions?'

The auto screeched to an angry halt. 'Please get off, madam,' the driver turned around and scowled. 'Look for another auto. I don't even want money from people like you.'

He was extremely rude. But I knew he wasn't really to blame. I had indeed taken him around on a crazy ride, unable to tell him to stop where I wanted to go: the beach. Yes, I wanted to visit the beach where Veer had first taken me upon my arrival in Mumbai. It was there that I had vented about Sharmila and her poor literary choices. Maheen and I had initiated an awkward friendship there, with the setting sun behind us. This was the beach where Veer had held my hand and told me that he loved me. But it was there that my fairy tales had been turned to dust, dissolved and annihilated by the darkness. That night sucked the peace out of me on that very beach. Yes, indeed. The dark is demonic and the demonic is real.

'Are you deaf? Have you escaped from a mental asylum? Get out right now!' The driver was quickly losing his cool. He made as if to pull me out, but I reacted quickly and slapped him hard.

'How dare you!' He growled, trembling with rage. 'You maniac! You bloody rich people! If you think so highly of yourself, go and buy a car. Just get out of my auto!'

The auto-driver was yelling so loudly that some people walking by stopped to see what was happening. They considered us with curiosity: an angry driver and a nervous, sweating woman. 'What happened?' one of them enquired. 'Why are you fighting?'

'This woman has been taking me around like a headless chicken for hours. And when I asked her to get out, she slapped me.'

Some of the spectators sighed heavily; a few shook their heads in disgust. 'What is this behaviour, madam? Do poor people not deserve respect? You think that auto-drivers are not human?'

As more people joined, my muscles started tensing up. Relax, I told myself. Such things are common in cities. But no, the mob was closing in around me. They wanted to grab me and pin me to the ground. Angry faces would slash my skin; powerful hands would strangle me. It couldn't be. Was this happening or was I having a nightmare? It had become impossible to differentiate fact from imagination. In a wild fit, I shoved the driver aside and started running.

'What happened to her? Why is she running?' I heard someone ask, unable to make sense of my behaviour. 'Perhaps she is mad,' someone tried to reason. I could not take issue with that. 'She shouldn't be allowed to roam around freely like this.'

I ran through the rush-hour traffic, sweat drenching my body, my legs aching. I was feeling short of breath; my heart felt like it was going to burst. I must have taken half a dozen wrong turns and alarmed many people on my way, but there it finally was: my home. I took the stairs all the way to the twentieth floor. As soon as I entered my apartment, I slammed the door shut, sank to the floor and wept.

After several minutes, I managed to stop crying. I realized my bones were aching terribly, but life seemed to be slipping back into me. Looking around the house, I reprimanded myself for going out in the first place. Home is safe, and I shouldn't have challenged myself.

'Meera!' A familiar voice called out from inside the house.

'Where had you been? What have you done to yourself? I was so anxious.'

It was Veer. He must have been waiting for me in the apartment. I was overjoyed to see him, but in my exhausted state, I couldn't bring myself to respond. For a second, I opened my mouth to speak. But then I decided to let him talk. It had been a long time since I had heard his voice. The sound of it soothed some of my wounds.

'Are you all right, Meera?' Veer clasped my hands in his. 'Why are you breathless? I have been waiting for you for so long. You have no idea the things that have gone through my head in the past few hours. Why didn't you take your phone?'

I sipped the cool water he handed me and felt some of my energy return. It wouldn't do to tell him the whole truth; he was already so fretful.

'Sorry, Veer,' I apologized. 'I couldn't find an auto, so I walked all the way home. There's nothing to worry about.'

'What? You know the doctor has advised you not to exert yourself. Really, Meera, you behave like a child sometimes.'

I shrugged, trying to act casual. Both of us wanted to say a lot more, but we swallowed our feelings. Our conversations were still a little strained; after all, the events of that night still hung heavy over us. He had professed his love for me repeatedly in the past few weeks. But our togetherness was still in its infancy.

'Shall I make you a cup of tea?' He volunteered, standing up. 'Or do you want to eat something? What about your favourite kadhi chawal?'

In his efforts to cheer me up, Veer had made me several cups of tea in the past few weeks. He had cooked piping hot dal, too, claiming it was comfort food. While I adored his affection, he had become absent-minded. The tea was always too sweet, the dal too bland.

'Shall we sit in the balcony for a while?' I changed the subject.

'Sure,' Veer smiled, grabbing a pack of cigarettes from the side-table.

※

Rings of smoke from Veer's cigarette hovered over my head. He was sitting by himself in the easy chair that I had placed in the balcony—the same chair that had seen the two of us jostle for space. He had tried to cosy up to me, but I had always resisted. It had become a kind of routine for us. I had even grown to like it. However, Veer didn't try anything of the sort.

'Ma had called,' I said, partly just to break the uncomfortable silence. 'She was asking when I was returning to Rishikesh.' I looked at Veer from the corner of my eyes, expecting him to stall me.

'She said that so many months have passed,' I continued when he didn't respond. 'Now I must return to help prepare for the wedding.'

Veer silently concentrated on his cigarette. What was the matter with him? Why wasn't he asking me to stay? After a long pause, he retorted, 'Do as you see fit. I mean, whatever suits you.'

His response alarmed me. No protests, no pleadings? Nonchalantly, he stood up and announced, 'Okay, I am heading to the kitchen to make some kadhi chawal. Trust me, it will be the best bowl you've ever eaten.'

I stared at Veer's receding figure as he walked into the kitchen. Down below, hundreds of cars were whizzing past. The moon, too, had hidden behind the clouds. Why was everyone leaving me alone?

Taking some deep breaths, I tried to get a hold on my emotions. It would be all right. Veer and I would get married soon and never have to be apart again. My wedding day could not come sooner.

※

I am not sure why I woke up at four in the morning. But as soon as my eyes shot open, I noticed that I was sweating profusely. In my hair—from the tips to the roots, behind my ears, on my neck—there was perspiration everywhere. I knew that I had forgotten to shut the bedroom window, but instead of a cool breeze, sweltering heat seemed to have invaded my house.

Getting up from my bed, I walked to the guest room. Veer was curled up on the sofa, snoring quietly. On the right corner of his lower lip, I could see a scab where a wound was healing. I settled on the floor near Veer and caressed his forehead. Something horrifying happened just then, almost making me scream. Blood spurted out of Veer's flesh, a few drops falling on my hand. As I looked on, frightened, his skin began to break in several places. Bruises covered his face, multiplying with every passing moment. How could this be happening? He had been perfect only seconds ago.

I tried to wipe off the blood with my dupatta while trying not to panic. But the more I wiped, the worse his bruises became. He stirred in his sleep and I, not knowing what to do, hid under the sofa. I felt guilty for disturbing his peaceful slumber. I rushed to my room, but Veer had woken up. Silently, he followed me, oblivious to his bloodied face.

But what was this? Instead of my bedroom, I had walked to the balcony; the easy chair was rocking in the strong wind. Without a word, I climbed out onto the ledge. Veer reached out toward me, but I was a woman possessed. I jumped. From the balcony of my flat on the twentieth floor my body plunged down the high-rise building in slow motion, past a few illuminated apartments full of startled people, on the fast track to hell. Just then, a veil seemed to cover my eyes. Was I dying? Or was I dead already?

My body landed in the abyss. I was instantly surrounded by a mob. Everyone was laughing hysterically. I tried to sit up and massage my throbbing head, but the crowd turned into a giant swarm of leeches and attacked me. It was at that point that I awoke screaming. The terror of the night had seeped right into my soul. It wouldn't take much for it to transcend the world of make-believe and become reality.

Convinced that I was truly awake this time, I looked around the room. The bedroom window was open and I could see the easy chair rocking in the wind. Veer was sleeping on the sofa outside. He hadn't shut the bedroom door but had honoured my wish to sleep alone before getting married. Had I been riding the high horse over something insignificant? Was it important to preserve one's virginity for one's husband? How necessary were those rituals of marriage to sanctify the love of two people? Nothing I had said or believed seemed to bear much meaning any longer. I wanted to go back in time to when Veer had held me tight. But instead of resisting, I would have wrapped my arms around him. He would have kissed me and unclothed my body lovingly and showered me with his love. We would have made love to each other.

That fateful night had shattered my beliefs, spat on my

face and made a mockery of what I thought 'virtues' were. Everyone preaches about having a clean and untouched body in order to be virtuous, no one says anything about having a clean soul. For most, virtues are only skin deep. And now that I was no longer a virgin, who was to say that I was virtuous?

Veer was sleeping under the bright lights of the living room. I wanted to walk up to him, turn off the lights and stroke his forehead. He cared about me so much, but I rarely expressed my love for him. I was terrified of repeating the events in my nightmare. I didn't trust myself to separate reality from imagination.

I wiped the sweat from my brow and looked around suspiciously. Was someone hiding in the apartment, waiting for an opportunity to pounce? The grey curtains were fluttering ever so slightly, but I hadn't the courage to look behind them. Gosh, who was this massive coward? I didn't like her at all. I longed to flee to Rishikesh, to go back to the riverbanks where I could walk fearlessly.

※

Veer entered my room to wake me at seven the next morning. I buried my face in a pillow, pretending to be asleep. I wanted to tell him that I had barely slept. I wish he knew that I had been searching for him in my nightmare, but he hadn't been around. I wanted him to know that if he pulled me close I would not resist. I would burrow into his chest and weep all my sorrows away.

But Veer made no attempt to draw me close. He sat next to me on the bed, idly gazing out of the window. Deciding suddenly to follow my heart, for the first time, I held his hands and embraced him, holding him to me tightly.

That morning, for the first time, Veer carefully pushed me away.

※

I sat alone in my bedroom that evening, surrounded by heaps of paper. My breath stank, and so did my spirits. I had consumed alcohol for the first time in my life. I had been tearing some irrelevant papers for half an hour. I shredded a wall calendar. Every morning, I would spend a few minutes assessing the painful passage of the days. As the days flew by, I slipped into irreversible cowardice. The calendar presented a truth I had no desire to face. It showed me the date of my marriage. My heart was trying to tell me that Veer was hiding his true emotions. I had to destroy the calendar before it destroyed my sanity.

I knew I had always mattered to Veer; he still valued me. But something had changed after that disastrous night. He cared for me much more but hardly ever met my eyes. He could not bring himself to kiss me on the lips—and no, it wasn't because he feared my resistance. Veer had stopped talking freely but he was a patient listener. I missed the days when he would talk for hours and I would soak in the details of his exciting life. I missed the stubborn child in him.

As I continued tearing at the shreds of the calendar, I remembered the black dress. When we had gone to the party at Joe's house, how miffed he had been because I hadn't worn it! On New Year's Eve, I had finally found the courage to wear that low-cut, off-shoulder dress but with a scarf wrapping my bare shoulders. This was the dress that was butchered and torn on the cold sand.

The sight of my bare shoulders no longer petrified me. I had stitched the torn edges as best I could, believing that this would put the pieces of my soul together. I wore the dress again without the scarf and tied my hair in a bun exactly like that night, just how Veer liked it. But why was I doing this? Why was I revisiting that night? Why on earth did I wear this dress again? I was unable to burn this dress or throw it away when I should have. Even days after that dreadful night, the image of me wearing that dress on the beach had lodged itself in my mind. I longed to face it, fight it and finally kill that image in my mind forever.

A voice in my head said, 'Deleting the undesired chapters of your life will not bring healing. Rewriting them with courage, instead, might save some part of you'.

I was still sitting on the floor when Veer walked into the room unannounced. I have never liked his habit of entering the apartment without ringing the bell. But that evening, I felt a bizarre sense of relief. Veer and I belonged to each other and this is why I did not mind it. I smiled and tried to stand, but my legs gave way and I stumbled.

'What on earth is this?' Veer screamed. 'Meera? Why? Why!' He fumbled, 'Why have you worn this shit?'

I blinked in confusion. My thoughts were racing and I could not get a handle on them. So, this is what it felt like to be drunk. 'Is this not your favourite dress? Listen to me, there is a reason I wore it, I need your help,' I began.

Veer didn't let me finish. 'Shut up, Meera! How can you do this to me?'

He was sobbing. It was the first time I had ever seen him cry. How fateful that it was me who had brought on those tears! I had reopened his deepest wounds. I tried to stand up straight again.

'Have you been drinking?'

I wanted to say, 'Yes, you always wanted me to drink so today I did.' But instead I said, 'N-no,' I stammered. 'I haven't drunk any wine.'

My words were slurred. I had no idea that speech could become so incomprehensible under the influence of alcohol.

Veer shouted at me again, 'Are you deaf? Tell me if you have been drinking. What is wrong with you?'

He was disappointing me. Didn't he notice the flowers I had strewn on the bed? The scented candles all over the floor? Wasn't this the moment for which he had been waiting? All his attention was focussed on the fact that I had been drinking.

'What are you trying to prove, Meera? Why are you doing all this nonsense?'

I had no idea why Veer was getting so agitated. Or perhaps I did, but I continued lying to myself. I wasn't the one hurting him; I hadn't done anything wrong. In fact, I felt right after a long time. My heart was beating fast; my thoughts were all over the place.

I didn't detest alcohol now. I had come to realize the hollowness of my choices only when my life was falling to pieces. The alcohol had helped me soar in the skies when I was fumbling on the ground; it let me reach the shore when I was drowning in the abyss.

Suddenly, I embraced Veer and started kissing him. I kissed his forehead, lips, neck, chest, shoulders… He stood there, not protesting but not responding either. His face felt wet. When I stopped kissing him, I noticed that he was crying. The gaping distance that had existed between us all these months had widened even more.

'Meera,' Veer asked me again, his voice low and pained. 'Please answer my question. Why have you been drinking?'

'Ma is calling me to Rishikesh to prepare for the wedding. Tell me if I should go.' Veer hadn't said a word when I had asked him this question the first time. I wasn't convinced by his feigned nonchalance. Why wouldn't he give me a proper answer? What was he trying to hide?

'Tell me, Veer,' I enunciated slowly this time. 'Should I go or stay here longer?'

Veer wiped away his tears, turned his back to me and walked out the door. I stood there waiting for an answer that never came.

༄

Hours after Veer left, I sprawled on my bedroom floor again, tearing away at the dress and everything it signified. Finally satisfied, I collected the pieces of the butchered dress in my trembling hands and walked to the balcony. I threw the pieces at the dark sky. I felt a little lighter. I stood there in the twilight completely naked, facing the demonic dark sky with courage. The breeze caressed me. For the first time since that dreaded night I felt comfortable in my skin. I was not bothered if any stranger would get an eyeful from the neighbouring windows. All my life I had been using words like 'virtues' and 'virginity' interchangeably, advocating for a chaste body and a sensible wardrobe. But what I did not know then was that the strength of the immortal soul is far greater than the threads that make your clothes. Alas...all my fears had dissipated; all my notions about life had been transformed. What does a corpse have to fear anyway...or had I been born again?

You must allow fear to swallow you completely once. Then, when you emerge from it, you are born fearless. Fear is incapable of taking over you repeatedly. In that moment, wrapped only by the blue-black sky, I felt freedom. While that unfortunate night had unwrapped me, broken my bones, pulled me out of my mother's peaceful womb and dropped me into the unknown, it had also strengthened my soul and opened my consciousness to a new reality.

Later that night, I lay in bed unclothed, not even covered by a blanket. I left the windows open to let the breeze in. For the first time in several nights, I felt drowsy. My eyelids drooped. Before I knew it, I was fast asleep. That night, I understood why we are born naked.

※

I woke with a massive headache. The sunlight streaming in through the window felt torturous. I got up lazily, wrapped myself in a bedsheet and drew the curtains. All over the room shreds of paper and cloth were fluttering about. Turning off the fan, I tried to piece together the events of the night before. It was a struggle, but I concentrated as best as I could. The memory of Veer weeping was the first to return.

I hurriedly dressed in a salwar-suit and called Veer. A robotic voice announced, 'The number you are trying to reach is not available at the moment.' My heart sank.

The doorbell diverted my attention. The courier-boy had come to deliver my train tickets to Rishikesh. Ma had sent me tickets for 25 February so that I could get at least ten days to prepare for the wedding. I stared at the envelope before carefully placing it in a drawer.

After showering, I stood before the mirror to dry my hair. Behind me was the temple that I had ignored. I had not tended to it in over a month. It was time to change that. With stiff steps, I walked to it and started cleaning with a dust-cloth. I washed the lamp, poured some oil in it, readied a cotton wick and struck a match. But before I could light the lamp, the small flame went out. Was this a sign, or was I just hesitant to revisit my faith?

And then, another notion entered my mind: that Mahadev did not want an unchaste woman to light a lamp for him. Well, who would judge if I was unholy or he was guilty? Our relationship had gone through immense turmoil in the last couple of months. I did not believe that lighting a lamp could salvage this failing connection.

Three days passed. Veer was not responding to my calls. Whenever I tried to reach him, his phone was either switched off or unavailable. Since I was leaving for Rishikesh soon, his silence made me disproportionately uncomfortable. Why had he abandoned me like this? I thought about visiting him at his home, but the prospect of meeting his mother daunted me. What if she sensed the reality I was struggling to hide?

Veer had convinced me to go about my life silently; I had agreed. There was no reason not to and I completely understood his point of view. Veer was a popular radio jockey and had a large fan following. Burying that night in the dark recesses of our hearts would be best for the both of us. After all, life wasn't going to stop. What good would it do for us to reveal the nasty details of that night? Some people would express grief; others might make us feel uncomfortable. Either way, they couldn't do anything about the fact of it.

So, no one knew anything of the horrific rape. Things were moving exactly as they had been a month ago. Why, then, had I been abandoned? Where had everyone gone? I had not exchanged a single word with Joe or Maheen or Kalika in what seemed like ages. Were they avoiding me? Had Veer confided in them about that night?

'One must keep a layer of dignity to be able to look the world in the eyes. The outside world should stay outside. It shouldn't be allowed to peep inside.' Veer had said.

I know that nothing had changed in the lives of the men who had raped me. They might have even forgotten about the incident. Unlike me, they couldn't care less about how dark the night had been, how loud my shrieks, how helpless my naked body. None of them lost sleep over my black dress stained with blood. They might even joke about spitting on me and breathing into my nose with their rancid, stinking mouths.

The doorbell rang again. I rushed to answer it, hoping desperately that it would be Veer. It wasn't.

'Where have you been? No phone calls either? I cannot even trace Veer.'

Joe was standing at the door, her face full of questions. While I was disappointed, I also felt pleased to see someone I knew.

'N-no, everything is fine,' I said carefully. 'I thought you might be busy...' I wanted to ask her to come inside but hesitated. It was strange but her presence unnerved me. The walls of my flat had witnessed so many things lately that I was afraid Joe might catch wind of them.

'Hey! What is this on your forehead?' Joe's question took me back to that dreaded night. I hid my fear and lied, 'Oh, I fell in bathroom. How have you been?"

'Well, won't you even invite me in?'

'Oh! Please. Come, come.' I managed a watery smile.

Joe was about to step in when the door of the other flat opened. Maheen, holding a dustbin in her hand, stared at us. I expected her to greet me, but to my surprise, she emotionlessly gaped at the both of us. 'Arey Maheen,' I called out, 'I haven't seen you in forever. How are you doing?'

She did not reply but stood rooted to her spot, staring at Joe. Her eyes seemed moist, or was that my imagination? I glanced at Joe. Surprisingly, she too seemed stunned. Both women looked shell-shocked. Before I could make sense of it, Maheen disappeared inside her apartment. Joe hurried to the elevator, without even a goodbye. 'Where are you going, Joe?' I shouted after her. 'Come back!'

But Joe did not stop. As soon as the elevator arrived, she stepped inside and vanished.

Why had the two of them behaved so peculiarly? Veer, too, had been missing for so many days. What on earth was going on?

My phone buzzed. Much to my amazement, it was Joe. 'Hello! What is up with you? Why did you leave so abruptly?' I waited for her to respond, but all I heard from the other end was sobbing.

'Joe?' She was making me anxious. 'Please, tell me what has happened. Why are you crying? Is everything all right?'

She continued crying, her sobs becoming hysterical. A lump formed in my throat. 'Has something happened to Veer? Please, Joe, say something!'

I was frightened. I had never seen her so helpless before. Deciding there was only one way to lay my fears to rest, I hung up and rushed to Joe's apartment.

※

'Everything is over, Meera. Things will never be the same again,' Joe wailed.

Joe—extremely drunk—had been weeping bitterly for over an hour. Her home was a mess: wine bottles lay everywhere, the air was foggy with cigarette smoke, the windows seemed like they had not been opened in weeks. What she had revealed to me had left me dumbstruck. Each word she had said hit me like a drop of acid, slowly eating away at my insides. Only a few hours ago, when Joe had left wordlessly, I had been eager to console her. But now that I knew, all I felt was heartache and a desperate urge to forget everything I had heard.

I held her hands and tried to bring myself to placate her. She looked at me through bloodshot eyes. It was difficult for me not to judge her actions. I was also furious with Maheen for behaving the way she had. Maheen was another well-trained slave who had been brainwashed to bow down, hide in the dark and obey blindly. Now I knew why her door had remained shut since the beginning. Had she done anything at all since her wedding other than shutting out the world? Joe's plight filled me with frustration.

'I did not know that Jahangir lived in the flat opposite yours, Meera,' Joe wiped her tears and managed to meet my eyes. 'When I suddenly saw his wife there, I nearly fainted.'

'I want her to forgive me,' she went on. 'I feel choked. Her tears from that night follow me wherever I go. She didn't say a word to me! Not one word of complaint or abuse! How could she behave like that?' Her voice was becoming more helpless as memories of the night filled her eyes. 'Meera, why didn't Maheen yell at me? If I had been in her shoes, I would have slapped myself hard! But she only stared at us woefully, as if I was snatching away her only hope of survival.'

'Let me pour you some water.' I poured some into a glass and offered it to her. It was better than sitting there like a statue.

'Meera,' Joe drained the water and looked at me pleadingly, 'please say something or I will go insane!'

'What do you want me to say?'

Joe sighed in frustration. 'Sleeping with men is not a big deal for me, Meera. Why, then, has sleeping with Jahangir become such a big deal that I am struggling to breathe? Is it a crime to dream big? I cannot orchestrate my own success; I have to depend on those who have taken the path before me. Why do people make such a big deal of sex?'

'You don't think it is a big deal?'

'Okay, tell me this,' Joe took a few deep breaths to calm down and continued. 'How is sex related to feelings? You love Veer, right? If he never touches you, will your love fade away? It won't, right? Love does not need sex to exist; sex is only a physical desire.'

Joe continued, 'Meera, I know that I am no intellectual, but why do I feel so guilty? It's almost as if I destroyed Maheen's soul.'

As Joe blabbered on, I found myself shaken to my core. Her outburst had shaken my beliefs. Had she asked me these questions a few weeks ago, I would have waxed eloquent about the all-encompassing beauty of love, the importance of having a chaste body and the definition of virtue. Even a small matchstick could dispel the darkness out of rooms, I would have told her. But now I knew that a matchstick burns only until the stick exists; the dawn dares to remain only until dusk arrives.

I stayed quiet. I could not preach to her now. I was nothing but an example of misguided optimism and shallow morals. I was masquerading as a woman who had it together while, in reality, my life was in shambles.

Despite the superficiality I often perceived in Joe, she was right about the emotional depths of love. Yes, my soul would love Veer forever even if our bodies never met. It was unnecessarily prudish of me to link love and sex so closely.

However, there was something I still failed to understand. If the body and the soul indeed exist on different planes, why did my heartache from that doomed night transcend everything? When so many hands had pinned me down and violated my body, why was it that I felt the scars on my soul?

Someone knocked on the door, forcing Joe to compose herself. I got up to answer it and found myself face-to-face with Kalika. Dressed in low-waist jeans, a red spaghetti-top and high-heels, she looked great.

'Oh, it is you.' She smiled at me. 'Such a pleasant surprise! I had actually come to visit Joe Didi. She was running a high fever yesterday.'

I think I stared at her too blankly because she began to re-introduce herself. 'Meera Didi, don't you recognize me? I am Kitty. Kalika, you know? We met here at the Christmas party last year.'

'Of course, I know who you are. Who could forget such a lovely doll?' I attempted to become a good host to prevent any more awkwardness. 'Would you like some water?'

'No, thank you.' She turned to Joe and frowned. 'Joe Didi, how dull you look! Didn't you go to see a doctor?'

'I am well, Kalika. Sorry, Kitty. That is your name now, isn't it?' Joe replied. 'Tell me, Kitty, why did you change your name? I used to ridicule my maid, who transformed from Leelavati to Laila. But look how many people she has encouraged!' Joe let out a sarcastic chuckle. 'By the way, how are your studies going?'

'Oh, don't worry about my studies,' Kalika shrugged. 'All that is just child's play.'

Joe looked at me with a strained expression. I jumped into the conversation, 'Kalika, would you like some tea?'

'My name is Kitty, not Kalika,' she scowled. 'I just told you.'

'Sorry, it was a slip of the tongue.'

'Never mind, Meera Didi. But yes, do make some tea for me while I use the bathroom.' She was quick to forgive, quicker to command. 'Could you add some cardamom?'

I must have been in the kitchen for around ten minutes, but the living room was very quiet. Kalika must still be in the bathroom, I thought as I walked out with the tea-tray. But there they both were, seated in a state of shock. Joe was holding Kalika's phone in her hands and staring at the screen in a daze. Kalika sat timidly on the floor, not meeting my eyes.

'What is up with the two of you?' I asked setting the tray on the table.

Joe passed Kalika's phone to me. On the screen was a text message that was evidently the source of the tension.

'Meet me at the hotel at 7 p.m. today,' the message read. 'This time, I will pay double the amount if you promise to double the fun...'

I could not read any further. I stood there, staring at the screen dumbfounded. It was overwhelming.

'What the fuck is this?' Joe screamed at Kalika. 'You got into prostitution? Why? You come from a decent family; you are studying in college... What happened to all that?'

Kalika, who had been cowering in a corner, flinched. As I stared at her, I remembered the girl I had seen several months ago. There had been an aura of innocence around that girl. Her hair had been tied in two unflattering braids and her salwar-suit was shapeless, but she had exuded a sense of dignity. Was that the same girl who sat before me with her head bowed? No, this was Kitty. I felt betrayed, as if I was witnessing a nightmare. Life was throwing curveballs at me and there was nothing I could do about it.

'I did not expect this from you, Kalika.' Joe shook her head disdainfully and started fiddling with the phone. 'I'll call your father right now and tell him everything. He will drag you back to your village! You do not deserve your freedom!'

In a flash, Kalika snatched her phone away. Her timidity had been replaced by rebellion. Enraged, she shouted back, 'I do not deserve freedom? Seriously, Joe?'

It was the first time I had seen Kalika speak to Joe so disrespectfully.

'I know everything about that friend of yours, that Jahangir! Is he your husband? Then why do you fuck him? I can see very well see what *you* do with your freedom!'

Joe was stunned. She could not believe her ears. The words stabbed at her when she already felt so frail.

'You bloody small-town scoundrel!' Joe shot back. 'Keep your filthy mouth shut! How dare you, a prostitute, talk to me like this?'

'Mind your language, Joe! I am not a prostitute. I'm a porn star.'

Joe blinked, disbelievingly. 'What did you say?'

'You heard me. I shall soon become a famous porn star, but you are doomed to remain a third-class model. We are both the same. I am sleeping with people for money and you do the same for modelling assignments. How is that different?'

The sound of a resounding slap filled the apartment. Joe was boiling by now. Her furious eyes betrayed how helpless she felt. Kalika, although taken aback, brushed her cheek lightly with her fingers and said, 'Why are you so offended, Joe Didi? You know the game. Everyone wants only this.' She pointed lewdly at her bosom. 'As for telling my father—well, first, tell *your* father what you are doing to land such big advertising campaigns. Then you can think of preaching to me.'

Kalika turned to me, clearly not done venting. 'Meera Didi, my naked body is worth its weight in gold. Veer Bhaiya must also want this from you, no? If you deny this pleasure to him, will he still love you? Will your marriage survive?'

Straightening her clothes, Kalika prepared to leave the apartment. 'Remember, Joe Didi,' she declared ominously before stepping out. 'If porn stars are filthy, the word 'star' would not have been attached to the title and people would not run after porn stars for their autographs. And I won't forget this slap. Soon, I will become bigger than you, and you'll be sorry that you treated me this way!'

Kalika slammed the door on her way out. Joe started sobbing helplessly. But I had no comforting words to offer. What on the earth had Kalika just said? Once again, I had been asked a question for which I had no answer. Although I knew I shouldn't have left Joe alone, I turned and left. My tears threatened to spill over at any moment. I didn't want Joe to see me in my drowning state.

※

I was so lost in my thoughts that I did not realize that the elevator arrived at the twentieth floor. I walked up to Maheen's door and started ringing the doorbell manically.

Maheen appeared at the door within minutes. 'Meera ji!' She cried in surprise, worried by my presence. 'It is ten in the night; you haven't slept yet? Why did you ring the bell so many times? I was terrified.'

Without responding, I walked into her house and sat down on the sofa. Maheen sat in front of me, her fists clenched and her eyes filled with anticipation. I did not stop to think about what my arrival would do to her; I only cared about myself. The chaos inside me was eating away at my nerves.

'Why didn't you go out shopping again?' I asked as I looked right in the eye.

Maheen must not have expected such a direct question. She tried to answer. 'My husband works hard to earn money. I figured I should not spend it so lavishly. You have come at this hour of the night to ask me this?'

'Tell me, Maheen,' I shot another question at the poor girl. 'Did your life get better after you bought that lingerie and frock?'

Maheen's lower lip quivered. 'Meera ji, why are you asking me all this?'

'Why did you get so distressed when you saw Joe at my door this morning?'

This was too much for Maheen. Her face paled and she started blabbering. 'I had put the milk on the stove to boil... It might have spilled...'

'Really? Doesn't the reason have more to do with the fact that Joe and your husband work together and sleep together?'

'He must be on his way home, Meera ji,' Maheen pleaded, her eyes filled with tears. 'Please leave.'

'Maheen, doesn't your Quran say that Allah is one and no one can be granted his status? Why then do you treat your husband like God?'

She tried to sit but fell to the floor and covered her eyes. I sat down beside her. 'Listen to me, Maheen. You are perfect. It is not your fault but that of your husband. He lacks a sense of commitment, and is unaware of the true definition of beauty. You needn't run around trying to please him; it is not going to work.' I had never been so forceful and blunt.

'You are mistaken,' Maheen shivered, firmly clinging to her notions. 'Nothing of this sort has happened.'

'Okay, if I am mistaken, then stop looking down at the floor and meet my eyes.' I don't know what had come over me, but I felt a deep anguish for everyone who pretended to be alive, for those who were too scared to face the truth. The one I hated the most was my own hypocritical self.

'A husband provides food, clothes and shelter, which is why a woman must never forget her duties towards him. This is what you have been parroting all your life, isn't it? Well, are you an animal?' I hissed at her, fury possessing me. 'Don't you need anything beyond that? How can you live like someone's doormat? Don't you have any self-respect?'

I have never spoken so venomously to anyone before. What right did I have to condemn Maheen's life, her beliefs and her reason for living? Perhaps, I reasoned much later, I had the right because our lives were connected. Just like the tsunami that does not differentiate when it drowns all that stands in its path, had the actions of those around me affected my destiny? Could I deny that the men who had raped me had permanently altered the course of my life? Had Joe's actions not affected Maheen? Were Kalika's desires her own or shaped by the aspirations of those around her? As a woman, I thought I had the right to say to another woman what I thought of her.

Maheen, who had started weeping while listening to my outburst, wiped her tears. She spoke softly, weighing her words with care. 'Meera ji, I have studied in a madrasa. If I lead my life as commanded by my faith and do not question its teachings, I will be blessed with eternal happiness. Yes, my husband does not love me here, but I will be loved in heaven. I don't want to argue about this with you as that would be the same as questioning my faith. You asked me how I chose to live in the dark, behind closed doors. Well,' she looked around her house and sighed, 'I don't have the strength to face the scorching reality outside these walls. Since I have failed to build a heaven in this life, I wish to go to the one Allah has created for me.'

I shook my head in dismay. How could I give this woman strength when I was so lacking in it myself? Strength comes from facing the truth; it doesn't come to someone who lies in a coffin and prays for death. I wasn't furious with Maheen anymore, but I was more distressed than ever.

The doorbell rang and I could feel a quick sliver of panic go up Maheen's spine. 'I think he has arrived.'

Jahangir walked into the house, stopping in his tracks when he saw me. '*As-Salaam-Alaikum*,' he greeted me politely. Behind his affable smile, I could see that he detested this intrusion.

'Please excuse me,' I quickly collected my phone and walked toward the door. 'Maheen, I am sorry for disturbing you at this hour. Good night.'

Maheen nodded slightly, desperate for me to leave. However, I was so stubborn that night, that I couldn't help turning to Jahangir and saying, 'Allah, an ocean of love and kindness, does not teach terror and slavery, which you have inflicted on your wife.'

Jahangir looked furious. I wanted to say much more, but

decided to leave them behind in the dark. I was a woman on a mission: it was time for me to face the burning sun. I had to face my own truths. Words might bring me the elusive peace I had been hunting for. I remembered the voice that has whispered into my ears, 'Deleting the undesired chapters of your life will not bring healing. Rewriting them with courage, instead, might save some part of you'.

※

I had forgotten the comfort that came with writing in my journal about all the conflicting emotions that were going through my head. I had been writing for hours. I took a break and saw that it was late; it seemed to be the longest night of my life. I looked at the white marble-floor of my apartment. Gosh, how dirty it was! I hadn't cleaned my house in weeks.

Feeling tired, I decided to rest and make sense of my random, somewhat claustrophobic thoughts. I saw myself standing on a vast sheet of ice. I was naked and the winds were freezing. Suddenly, I slipped into a pool of icy water. Death was circling me. Out of nowhere, Joe, Maheen and Kalika appeared and pulled me out of the pool. As I crouched on the bank heaving deep breaths, I caught sight of my reflection in the clear and undisturbed surface of the water. I went as close to it as I could. But then, my eyes shot open.

I hadn't even begun to analyse the strange dream when I heard a voice calling out to me. Sitting there with miserable eyes was Veer.

'Veer!' I screamed, elated. 'What are you doing here? Where have you been?'

'I was worried,' he replied, averting my gaze. 'I could not wait for daybreak.'

'Oh? You were worried about me after so many days? How come?' I finally complained. Ever since the evening when I had finished a whole bottle of wine, Veer had abandoned me. I was seeing him after what felt like an eternity.

Veer did not reply, fidgeting with things around the room awkwardly. His eyes fell on my journal, open to the latest page. Picking it up, he turned the pages and read. Then, turning towards me, he yelled, 'What's all this, Meera? What rubbish are you writing?'

'Rubbish?' I could not understand why Veer was losing his temper. How was it wrong to pen my emotions in my journal? I was doing it only to find some solace.

'I was right! You have indeed gone mad!' Veer threw the journal on the floor. 'Your mind is still swimming in the thoughts of that filthy night. You are reliving it through these writings. Do you know why I didn't visit you for so many days? It's because your insanity is driving me nuts!'

Veer's words delivered a punch to the gut. Where had his love gone? 'My madness?' I repeated. 'No, Veer, I will tell you why you didn't visit me for so long. It's because you detest seeing my face. Your fiancé, someone you 'own', was violated by another. It is this that you cannot stand!'

He was quiet but I continued screaming. 'All these days, you have been running away from the truth. But you think you are sane. And I, the one who lives with this truth every waking moment, has lost it. Excellent, Veer!'

Beads of sweat formed on my forehead. I hadn't known the extent of my fury. It was only when I voiced my emotions that I realized what I genuinely thought about Veer.

'Veer, whenever you see me, you are reminded that those men unclothed me before you could. They saw me naked before you could. My unchaste body reeks of filth but only to you. Isn't that right?'

'Meera!' Veer screamed in anguish, and I realized I had finally said too much. 'Please, shut up right now! I cannot take any more of this.'

I had made him weep again. I, too, was weeping inside. I wasn't being vindictive. I assumed that inflicting injuries on him would heal mine.

Veer stopped crying and stood up, as if to leave. 'Where the hell are you going?' I roared, clutching the journal to my chest. Pouring my thoughts into it had brought me tremendous peace.

'Where can I go, Meera? Nothing I say matters to you anymore. But I will still urge you not to reveal everything. Books should be fictional, not about the gashes on one's own body.'

It clicked only then why Veer had gotten so agitated. He had assumed I would publish everything I had written in my diary. He didn't know that writing a book was the last thing on my mind; I had been scribbling away in my journal as a coping mechanism. 'I am not writing any book, Veer,' I laughed. 'This is my diary. You had stopped talking to me, and I had no one to turn to. So I poured my heart out on these papers…'

'Stop lying, Meera,' he interrupted. 'I can see it in your eyes. That bloody night has eaten away all your brains.'

That was enough. I didn't have the patience for this any longer. 'Yes, you are right,' I admitted. 'That night has destroyed my peace. And you would be lying through your teeth if you said that the darkness does not terrify you too!'

'Ah, so you admit it,' Veer smirked. 'You have reduced the

entirety of your life to that one night. Everything you used to stand for has been lost.'

'I agree. I am suffering every minute. And do you know who is to blame for this? You!'

Veer stared at me, completely clueless. My words plagued him. 'Meera, I don't know what has happened to you. I only know that this is our life, not a movie. I beg you. Come out of that dark world and live your life.'

'I cannot do that,' I hissed. 'My world collapsed long ago. I feel like a hypocritical, hollow person, surrounded by insensitive people like you!'

'What?! How dare you? What have I done to you?'

'Why are you so surprised? You were so desperate to fuck me. But now that I've been reduced to this shell of a filthy person, you finally have a reason to keep your distance. Isn't that why you fled the other night? Very conveniently you used the excuse that I was too drunk.' I knew I was burning bridges that might never be repaired, but whatever remained of our relationship was not going to last. I felt that it was best to get everything out in the open.

'Don't be absurd, Meera,' Veer spoke softly. 'I would never think that. I left because you were depressed and not thinking straight...'

'It's okay, Veer,' I brushed him away. 'Guess I always knew that you didn't love me. Before our engagement, you must have slept with many girls. And yet, you left all those beautiful, modern women to settle down with a small-town stranger. You were just happy to find a virgin to marry.'

Veer walked away and sat down in the farthest corner of the room. Desperately trying not to yell, he said, 'I am not going to indulge your absurdity.'

'Okay. Tell me this. Now that I have also slept with many boys and can give you a run for your money in philandering, do you still want to marry me?'

'Be quiet, Meera,' Veer muttered under his breath. I could see he was itching to slap me.

'What does rape feel like, Veer?'

It was a question I had wanted to ask him ever since he had ordered me to suppress the memory. It had not let me undress in peace even within the walls of my house. When I menstruated, I could smell the stench emanating from my vagina. It was an ache inside my soul—a clawing desire to undo the events of that night.

'Meera...' Veer could not look at me, but I saw the horror in his eyes.

'I will tell you what it feels like, Veer,' I held up his chin and forced him to look at me. 'It makes me feel like a dumpster on the roadside where anyone can spit, piss or unload their garbage. I am a rag doll that has been chewed, spat on and crushed. Do you remember how they laughed at me? And yet, the next day, you asked me to forget everything and remain silent for the rest of my life. I am bleeding from the inside and you wonder why?'

I knew that we would never come back from this, but I could not stop. All warmth and affection had been sapped from me; all that remained was agony. Yes, Veer must have suffered in silence too. But I wanted him to be honest. A riot of emotions flashed across his face.

After several moments, Veer pulled me close and whispered into my ears, 'Please forgive me, Meera. You are right; I have been hiding from you. But do you know why? It's because I cannot stand the disdain and hatred I feel for myself. I failed to protect you. All of it happened before my eyes! Meera, I don't have the strength to make those monsters pay for their sins. I cannot even do anything to heal your wounds. It makes me feel inadequate and bitter.'

Veer finally bared his heart to me. He had been suffering too, and the knowledge made me feel less alone.

'Meera, time will heal everything. It might seem impossible now, but with time, we will find the strength to deal with every misfortune. I don't want the world to know, Meera. If people find out, nothing will ever be the same. We will never be able to live peacefully. I don't want to ruin everything that we have.'

'Everything *is* ruined, Veer,' I said, disappointed in his reaction. Veer valued his image so much that he let his fear of shame control him; he did not want people to gossip about us. 'You think my body will ever stop stinking? Even if those monsters paid for their crime, my soul would still be stained. I am sorry, but there's nothing I can do about it.'

'Is that why you are writing a book?' Veer enquired, exasperated. 'To heal your soul?'

'For God's sake, Veer! I am not writing a book! I told you it's only my personal journal.'

'I know you are lying, Meera. Why don't you accept it?'

'You don't want to believe me. I can't say anything to convince you to change that.'

'Meera, there is no point in staying together if you don't respect me or my wishes at all.'

Listening to him, I wondered how long he had been waiting for an opportunity to say this. I had worked myself up beyond the point of no return. Even Veer's heart-breaking statement did not push me to make amends. His refusal to have any faith in me was a clear indicator of his unwillingness to be together.

'I agree, Veer,' I responded coldly. 'Let's not beat around the bush. I know that you don't want to marry me.'

'No! I did not mean that!' He held my hands once again and inhaled deeply. 'Meera, please don't do this to us. I am begging you.'

I pulled my hands free and took a step back. 'There is no "us" anymore. I have heard enough, Veer. Now it's time for you to hear me out.' I pointed to the door and turned away from him. 'Please leave. I have the train tickets for Rishikesh, but I will postpone my trip. You needn't worry about the rent; I will pay it myself.'

'Why are you doing this?'

He was begging. He brought his palms together in utter desperation. But my heart ached and I felt incapable of consoling him. I was choking and his presence in the room was making it worse. Veer and I were like fire and water. Only one of us could survive if we lived together. And I really wanted to live.

'Shut the door on your way out,' I told him and headed to the bedroom. When we aren't able to change a situation, we must change ourselves. And I was changing.

Meera Dares the Unthinkable

25 Feburary 2012

'We met in October last year, didn't we?'

Sharmila sat in front of me, smiling. I couldn't tell if she was being sarcastic. Yes, I had gone back to the same woman who had belittled and insulted me. The owner of Sharmila Publications had kicked me out a few months ago, calling my writing ridiculous and childish. And yet, here I was in her office.

'Yes, we did,' I replied, drinking water from the ridiculous silver chalice. Back then, I had been hesitant to even touch it. 'But I'm sitting here again with a new story, a real story.'

'Well, tell it to someone who's listening. I told you then, and I'm telling you now: I have no interest in your fanciful stories of heaven.'

'Yes, I do remember that you prefer publishing tales of hell. I have something for you along those lines.'

Sharmila stopped rocking her chair and glared at me. 'Not again, Meera. Aren't you crossing your limits?'

'Sharmila ji, to write about real hell, one needs to walk

through it. I promise that if you read my story, you will definitely experience a hellfire that's demonic. I remember what you told me: it is the demonic which sells,' I said. 'You won't be disappointed this time, I promise.' I handed her a thick bundle of papers, neatly spiral-bound.

Sharmila smiled calmly while flipping through the manuscript. After reading only the first few pages, she stared into my eyes and exclaimed, 'No rainbows? No sunshine? This definitely seems up my alley.'

I sat there for a long time as Sharmila skimmed through the pages. Her eyes became as large as saucers as the chapters progressed. 'This is excellent, Meera!' She paused and looked up.

'It is what you mentioned during our first meeting. Exactly the way you wanted. This might be a book-asm for some and a revelation to others—a real story hidden in the dark corners of life. It is soaked in lust, sins, desires and miseries.'

Sharmila listened without blinking. Finally, she said in a firm voice, 'We would like to publish this.'

I threw open the door as I walked out of the office with my head held high. That morning, I embraced the rising sun and left the dark behind. It felt terrific.

Time to Face the Music

March 2012

It is 6:30 a.m. The sun hadn't come up yet. The furious mob continues to protest outside my building. They have been here all night.

After talking to Ma, I had begun to feel more restless. I had been hoping that the news of all this chaos wouldn't reach her. Damn the television!

I had decided to scream at the world. I should have known that the world would shout back at me.

Hiding in my twentieth-floor apartment, I had nothing to do but wait for the anger of the mob to dissipate. What if I was murdered by this violent mob? I had only dared to tell the truth behind the closed dark doors. But it had brought misery to hundreds of people. No one ever wants to hear the truth. It is often unpleasant and shatters false hopes.

Once again, I check the windows and the doors. They are locked. Then, I turn the television on to a chaotic scene unfolding outside the office of Sharmila Publications. A horde of reporters have surrounded Sharmila and are shouting their questions at her. I can see the effort it takes for her to stay calm.

'Sharmila ji,' says a young woman, jostling with the others to find space, 'your publishing house is being called immoral because of the book *Roar of the Dark*. There have also been public burnings of the book. Why did you publish it?'

'Thousands of copies have sold already,' replies Sharmila, adjusting her sari. 'I am not worried about any loss. It's the people who haven't been able to understand the book who are at a loss. I appeal to the government not to ban this book.'

'Madam, many people feel that the author only wrote this book for cheap publicity.'

'No one needs to take up the laborious job of writing a book only for publicity,' Sharmila scowls at the reporter. 'Tell me, if a girl stands naked on the roof, would you make her famous and hound her for an autograph? Or would you reprimand her? I think you would make her famous overnight. In the grand scheme of things, there are many ways to get cheap publicity. But, for this author, writing a book was not one.'

I am surprised by Sharmila's reaction. How is it that she is on my side? Has my story impacted her in some way? Reality steels her resolve. On the other hand, it has made me mercurial. But she and I are stubborn. I am realizing this for the first time.

'I have a question for you, Sharmila ji,' says another reporter thrusting a mic in front of her. 'How can you justify an author who blatantly reveals details about her private life and endorses bedroom talk in the open?'

This is too much for Sharmila. 'Oh! What are *you* up to in private that you dare not bring out in the open? I gather that you have quite a lot to hide from your ridiculous question. You cannot even say the word "sex"!'

'So, you want everyone to dance naked on the roads?'

'Maybe you should try it once,' Sharmila responds sarcastically. 'It might help you shed your reservations and prudishness. Maybe then the word "naked" can rid itself of the shame and taboos that have become associated with it.'

'But madam...'

'No further comments,' says Sharmila as she gets into her car and drives off.

The reporter continues the telecast, strongly condemning the incident and the 'shameful' book. Each word that Sharmila said infused me with courage. I am ready to face whatever comes. Even death.

I pack my things into suitcases. There isn't much I want to take with me. I open the cupboard and my eyes fall on my favourite grey curtains. How good they used to make me feel! I decide to leave them behind. It wouldn't do to carry them with me to Rishikesh. They wouldn't let me overcome painful memories. Shades of grey and black don't appeal to me anymore. Now, I will look for new colours with which to fill my existence.

I also decide to leave behind the idol of Mahadev. All my life I worshipped him so that he could hold my hand and reassure me that the peaceful all-encompassing dark I believed in and the dark that he meditated in were the same. But he had betrayed my trust. Now, if I mattered to him, let him be the one chasing me. Let him appear in front of me to hold my hand.

ॐ

Today is 5 March. The date is printed in golden letters on the wedding card Veer had presented to me at Joe's party.

Thousands of people had been invited to attend the wedding and witness the union. My father used to say, 'Meera's marriage would be the biggest event in Rishikesh. Everyone would look at my daughter with envy.' Ironically, masses of people wait for me right outside the building, although the welcome they want to give me isn't what my father had in mind.

But I don't fear the mob anymore.

As I open the door and step out, pieces of dried chillies brush against my toes. Like Mahadev, these threads that I vested my faith in have also deserted me. I glance at Maheen's door, hoping to meet her one last time.

Surprisingly, the door to her apartment is open. I am worried about her. As soon as I step in, I know that something is wrong. All her things are thrown helter-skelter, including earrings, bangles and the black cloth with which she covered the television. I cannot see Maheen anywhere. I haven't seen her since that encounter with her husband. Had I made things worse for her? I push open the bathroom door. What I see leaves me petrified. On the floor is a knife. Near the knife is an open matchbox and a canister of oil. If disaster has a smell, I can feel its stench invade my nostrils.

A tired sob catches my attention. I breathe a sigh of relief when I see Maheen sitting on the floor. Quickly, I scan her from head to toe: no knife marks, no bleeding, no burns. She has not harmed herself in any way. Then what is she doing there and why is her home in a mess? Is it the screaming mob outside? Her husband? Or is it me who is responsible for her misery?

Maheen sees me only when I place my arm around her shoulders. She stares at me like a terrified child for a while and begins to howl. I feel the weight of guilt coming down on me.

'Please forgive me, Maheen!' I cry out, hugging her close to my chest. 'I shouldn't have talked to you like that. Did Jahangir say something to you? Did he hit you? Please tell me what happened.'

'Meera ji, it's nobody,' she manages to mouth a few mumbled words through her tears. 'It was me who threw all those things on the floor. I tore the black TV cover too. But I could not gather enough strength to pull the curtains away, to let the light in...' Maheen holds on to me tighter, shaking. 'You were right, Meera. I am too weak, too frightened. I don't have any self-respect...'

'No, Maheen, please don't cry,' I implore, wiping her tears. 'I am ashamed of everything I said to you and your husband. You are in this state because of me.'

Maheen continues as if she hasn't heard, her words distorted by her sobs. 'Meera ji, I want colours in my life. Why should anyone else make my decisions for me? I have never seen the God I believe in so much and the man I treat like God has never understood me. I am suffocating. I am such a coward that I could not even kill myself!' Maheen kicks the canister of oil.

With some difficulty, I help Maheen stand, take her to the bedroom and bring her a glass of water. She looks at me, hoping for consolation. But I feel like a bitter failure. Only a few minutes ago, I, too, had not dared to take my grey curtains with me. I hadn't broken away from my own dark fears either. The events of the past few weeks would stay with us forever.

'Maheen, you have to pull the curtains away. Only you can break open the doors that imprison you. But I promise that I will speak up for you today. Of that you can be certain.'

I don't think Maheen understands what I tell her, but

she nods and shuts her eyes. Before leaving, I shut the door so she won't be disturbed anymore. After all, peace is more valuable than pride.

My Last Scream

I had never intended to publish the pages from my personal diary. Veer would never know that he was the one who had inspired my actions. He had chosen his image. He had not wanted me to speak my truth. But I had chosen my healing over his image.

Today, as I stand alone on this podium, facing hundreds of people, I can sense that most of them see me with either pity or embarrassment. Some probably hide stones, ready to pelt them at me. The media is here for their next scintillating cover story. Some security personnel stand on guard to prevent the crowd from getting violent. Only a handful of faces in the audience seem to share my anguish.

I am worried about my parents who might be watching me on television. Briefly, I wonder, what if Veer had been right? Maybe some truths should be hidden. On that dreadful night, Veer had brought me home, hidden me from prying eyes. He had ordered me to suppress my emotions, to stay quiet no matter how much I ached inside. 'I care about your dignity,' he had explained. 'Silence will bring you tranquillity.'

But I knew the reality was different: he cared about *his* dignity; he wanted to preserve *his* peace. For several days, I had obeyed my fiancé. But neither had I found peace, nor had I been able to redeem my self-respect, which had been torn apart by those monsters. Why should I regret choosing my pride over his peace; my truth over his lie; my courage over his timidity?

The ones who injure the flesh are criminals, but the ones who wound the soul remain free.

On the table in front of me sits my book. Next to it is a glass of water. My hands shake as I lift the glass and drink from it. Today is my last opportunity to give voice to my wounds, to try to explain myself to a world that has turned against me.

I clear my throat and start reading.

Roar of the Dark

Chapter 1

When something happens in life
That shatters the castle of my dreams,
The skies fall upon me,
And so distant my dreams begin to seem...
The womb is dark. Shiva is dark.
You may fear the dark,
But in the dark, I thrive.

One evening, while standing at the seashore, I wrote these lines after I had been kicked out of the palatial high-rise office of Sharmila Publications. My bundle of fanciful stories lacked reality, I had been told. I dared to love the dark. My optimism was a rebel that always chose to deny the unpleasant. I was the

Brahma of my fanciful world. Feeling fearless, I was blissfully unaware of the 'reality' that would come barging into my life.

I have decided to read out a few chosen words from selected pages. So far, I have not taken my eyes off the book. The audience is quiet. Yet, I feel as if the stone-pelting might start at any moment. I decide that I must complete what I have begun.

Chapter 3

The woman was covered in black from head to toe. She peeped out at the sun through the dark curtains of her home. She hoped that the warmth of the sun would bring some cheer into her ice-cold house. If only Maheen had understood that it wouldn't do to peep through the curtains! The curtains had to be pushed apart and the windows thrown open for the light to dispel the darkness in her life.

The Greek philosopher, Aristotle, revered by society, once said, 'The relation of male to female is by nature a relation of superior to inferior and ruler to ruled.' I have no sympathy for Maheen. The one who does not stand up for herself deserves to remain a slave.

Chapter 4

Joe aspired to become a star. But to reach her destination, she had to walk through the storm. Who was the criminal here? Was it Joe who had stepped outside in a storm or was it the storm itself that had blocked the other paths of Joe's life? So engrossed was she in her ambitions that she didn't realize they continued to push her weak, poor soul into a deep trench. While Joe sold herself for heaven, Maheen begged for it. Both women betrayed themselves in their futile quest for paradise.

Chapter 6

A tiny fish used to live in a small pond. But she had big dreams: she wanted to swim in a big tank. One day, the fish slipped through a crack and into a stinking drain. She started panting, unable to breathe. When she noticed other fish swimming comfortably, she learned from them and picked up the art.

Kalika's story was no different. When she landed in Mumbai, she taught herself to thrive. Her schoolbooks had taught her the stories of women like Lakshmi Bai and Kalpana Chawla, who were celebrated for their valour and wit. However, she was disillusioned when she saw the real world chasing for the autograph of a woman who flaunted her curves.

I think the fault rested with Kalika and the hypocritical society in which we live. Indeed, she felt she had no choice but to swim as per the fancies of the other fish; otherwise, she would be a misfit who would either drown or become an outcast.

I dare to look up and see Sharmila sitting in the front row. The audience is staring at me; many of them look reproachful and unforgiving. I stare at them defiantly. I am not ready to forgive them either. They have no right to shush me. Sharmila had once told me, 'If people can't hear you speaking, then scream. If they try to ignore your screams, howl.' My faith in *Sanatan* teaches me: '*Nirbhaya Bhava*'. Be fearless. I take a deep breath and read from the next chapter.

Chapter 7

Throughout her life, Meera observed many fasts for Lord Shiva. Every evening, she lit a lamp in front of his statue asking him to appear in front of her someday. He did, that night, when the darkness engulfed her. She lay naked on the cold sand, her body mutilated and her soul shaken. And quietly, he witnessed the rape.

Why was Mahadev letting her suffer? The rapist was wearing a silver locket with Mahadev distinctly engraved on it; he must have been a devotee of Lord Shiva, too. Lord Shiva had been a mute spectator. On that night, Meera felt both her soul and her faith die.

'Shut your stinking mouth, you bitch, we don't want to hear the details of your sex life!' Someone shouts from the audience, stopping me mid-sentence. But I wouldn't stop. No, I must not be daunted.

Chapter 8

'Allah thus commands you concerning your children; the share of a male is like that of two females.' I sarcastically smiled and continued, *'Men are protectors and maintainers of women. Food, clothes and shelter are provided, in return for a lifetime of slavery. It is unbelievable that a woman's place in society is just above an animal.'*

'Silence yourself right now and don't you dare question our faith! Don't try to mislead our women otherwise there will be consequences,' shouts a voice. Several voices join him, hurling expletives. I know they can harm me, kill me; but I was reborn. And I am ready to die and be born a third time.

'Then the Lord God made a woman from the rib he had taken out of the man, and he brought her to the man.' I look up, fold my hands and ask the crowd, 'If it is man who birthed woman at the time of creation, then what changed? Why have women been given the charge of giving birth ever since?'

I grin sarcastically; I do not avert my eyes from anyone for possibly the first time since that night. I know that I will never be forgiven for my blasphemy, but it does not matter to me. God himself must weep when He sees what we do to his earth.

'Have you dared to pelt stones at the posters of that porn star, Hunny Jasmine, who objectifies and reduces a woman's worth to just their bodies—as meat for consumption?'

'Men, the supposedly superior beings, have dominion over every inch of God's creation but women are forced to hide themselves under black tents and can't even breathe fresh air peacefully.

'You bow down to Kamakhya Devi; but a bleeding woman can't even say aloud that she is menstruating. You should be raging against this instead of hurling abuses at me!'

'Stop your nonsense right now!' A middle-aged man cries out. 'You dare speak one more word and you will be dead!'

'You think too much of yourself!' Another man shouts, his face red with rage. 'You came here to live with a boy without marrying him and are now preaching to us about morals and culture?' He turns to the crowd and says, 'This girl is misleading our women. Kill her!'

The audience is angry. So many people have started screaming and protesting that I can no longer hear myself think. Something hits my forehead and blood oozes out. I collapse to the ground. The last thing I remember seeing is

Sharmila getting up from her chair and running toward me. Someone touches my shoulders. I must be dying. But I have never felt more alive.

Meera Meets Mahadev

My feet touch the sea waves; the water feels cool. It is still dark around me. I can see a few morning joggers in the distance. This beach has seen me rise to the skies and be dumped into the abyss. I stand here wearing my thick coat of armour once again.

Society prides itself on being civilized; it hates exposing all its hollowness and hypocrisy. That day, at the book reading, people threw stones and hurled abuses at me because they did not want me questioning their faith. They have manufactured a God who is like them—full of worldly emotions like anger, hatred, sexism and bigotry. They have written rule books in His name to suit their own personal agendas. When I pointed a finger at their misdeeds, they became furious. Many people felt that Meera, Kalika, Joe and Maheen lived out their destinies; that society could not be held responsible for what happened. They didn't want me to open the doors, because as long as the doors remained closed, the reign of the dark would continue.

That day, after the chaos at my book reading, I fell unconscious, only to wake up in Rishikesh. My parents were at my side. It was finally quiet. I stopped writing fictional stories. Instead, I busied myself in living in light of the truth.

But today, I am back in Mumbai for one important task: to bid farewell. I hadn't got the chance to say a heartfelt goodbye to the sea—my best friend, the silent spectator to my greatest joys and sorrows.

It has been nearly a month since I last spoke to Joe; I know she is angry with me. But I am relieved to know that she signed a few big deals after my book got published. It might have partly been due to the controversies caused by the book. Hopefully, she does not need Jahangir anymore. I always wanted her to soar in the skies. I know she can weather any storm.

Kalika prosecuted me for ruining her reputation and tearing apart her dreams. Her father took her back to Haryana and put an end to her ambition of becoming a famous porn star.

Maheen, too, slammed the door in my face when I went to visit her, but not before slipping a small note into my hand. It said, 'Thank you for speaking my truth. I never wish to see you again. I choose peace over pride, faith over truth and heaven over earth.'

Their fury is well-founded, I know. What right did I have to reveal their stories to the world? After having dealt with me, the crowd must have pelted stones at the three of them. I was too proud of my courage to stop and think about the consequences for anyone else.

But I *had* to open the doors. If all of us get comfortable living under lock-and-key, the darkness will continue to spread. Someone has to let the light in. Not all of us have the keys to unlock the doors in our lives. But we must try to break free.

I turn on my pocket radio and listen to the news. '*The police have started an investigation into the heinous gang-rape which happened in Mumbai on New Year's Eve. One of the criminals has been caught with the help of his description which was given by the victim. He was also wearing an engraved Shiva locket. The hunt for the criminals is on. The state government has also made a statement saying that the rest of the absconding rapists shall be caught and punished.'*

The radio jockey suppressed some of his usual cheer while sharing the news. *'Meera Thakur's controversial book,* Roar of the Dark, *has been banned. Orders have been issued to remove all copies of this book from bookstores. However, the owner of Sharmila Publications claims that millions of copies have already been sold and that she will go to court against the ban. Meera Thakur has been missing for a month.'*

I turn it off and stare back at the rising saffron sun. The sunlight floods the beach. I see my bag lying on the sand. Inside, I have packed the grey curtains and the idol of Mahadev I had left behind in the flat. I had constantly asked myself why that demon who obliterated my soul was wearing Mahadev on a pendant around his neck. I realized that since Mahadev had witnessed his sin, he would make sure to bring the criminal to justice. I smile and gather a fistful of sand. Then, I let it go while apologizing to Mahadev for the words I spoke in rage.

ॐ

'Please take me to Mumbai station,' I request the auto-driver. As I get in, I suddenly feel as if I am being watched. Someone is standing across the road looking at me. It is Veer. My heart skips a beat, but I don't react. After the the book reading, a video had gone viral. It showed people pelting me with stones. The hand that had held me before I passed out had belonged to Veer. He had protected me again, carrying me away from the mayhem. And here he was again, ensuring my safe return to Rishikesh. Why doesn't he come to meet me? Does he need more time? I know we will find a way to get back to each other someday.

'How far is the station?' I asked the auto-driver.

'Madam, it will take an hour.'

I nod and make myself comfortable. Suddenly, in the rear-view mirror, I catch sight of the auto-driver and my heart stops cold. The reflection is unearthly: it has long hair and its skin is blue. It is Mahadev.

I blink. *Don't be ridiculous*, I reprimand myself. *Would Mahadev ever drive an auto to take me to the station?* Yes, he could. I live in a world he made. Sometimes, I have come to realize, liberation is bestowed upon you disguised as misfortune. I smile, because I know now that the voice which constantly whispers words of guidance to me in times of desperation belongs to him. Yes, I may have complained to him and about him, but we take these liberties only with those we consider our own. It is a rainbow of experiences that helps us to become 'Shiva' from 'Shava'. Upon my return to Rishikesh, I will give Ma and Pa a big tight hug.

Nirbhaya Bhava. Be fearless.

Acknowledgements

My *isht*, Lord Shiva; I cannot imagine any part of my life where he is not a guiding presence.

My family is my strength and the source of my audacity. They teach me to exist above gender, think beyond survival and question the forbidden.

I cannot express the depth of my gratitude to Kapish Mehra and Rupa Publications for trusting in my story and guiding me throughout this journey.

I am indebted to Deboshree and her superb literary skills which have helped shape this book immeasurably. I also want to thank Saswati and Wesley for helping me through the process. I would like to thank Nishtha for her constant warmth and support.

There are so many others who have helped me through life, who love me. I am grateful to each one of you.